Stallion of the Sands
by Helen Griffiths

Lothrop, Lee & Shepard Co., New York

By The Same Author

Horse in the Clouds
Wild and Free
Moonlight
Africano
The Wild Heart
The Greyhound
The Wild Horse of Santander
Leon

For Adults
The Dark Swallows

A WORLD FAMOUS HORSE STORY LIBRARY Selection

Contents

Part I Pampa Stallion

The Foal 7

Grass and Sunshine 16

Yearling 25

Pampa Fire 35

Gauchos 43

Terror 50

The Lonely Beach 58

Part II The Boy

Aurelio 70

In Pursuit of a Dream 77

Santa Clara 86

Lessons and Legends 97

The Hunt 105

Land of Mists 113

The Parting 121

The Sand Stallion 127

An Outlaw's Story 135

The Indian's Way 144

The Return 152

Part I

Pampa Stallion

The Foal

On a bright day in early spring the albino colt was born. There was nothing to differentiate him from the other half-a-dozen colts born during the same day, except his coloring. The others were bays and duns with frizzy black tails and manes, and perhaps a white splash on the face or legs. There were two red-and-white foals with hides dappled like cloud shadows on the grass. Only the albino was the color of the spring cloud itself, touched with the pink of sunset.

Snow white was his woolly tail and brushy mane; snow white the fluffy hair that thickly covered him. And pink were his lips and nostrils and all his flesh, and the eyes that opened wonderingly.

In everything else he was like the others, a gangling bundle of bone and damp skin at birth, shivering on the soft earth while his mother pummeled warmth into him with soft and busy muzzle. The light and the air and the scents all about him were overwhelming in the first seconds of his life. Stiff and trembling, he clung to the earth until warm blood began to pulse through his veins. The clouds faded from his eyes, and his lungs took on an even rhythm.

Then the air was no longer a cold force, crushing him; and the light no longer hurt or bewildered him. His stiff legs began to kick, his big ungainly head to twist about. Within seconds he was lying upright, his legs more or less gathered under him. For the first time, he was taking a look at the world.

All he could see was grass and the long solid legs of his mother. He could smell the freshness of the grass, and he could smell the warm, sweaty scent of his mother. He knew instinctively that she was his dam, his strength, the key to his existence, and his first outstretchings were toward her. The pink muzzle touched at her legs, wrinkling as it did so. The mare's head came close, big and comforting.

She whickered softly, and the colt grunted in answer, moving his head convulsively in his first efforts to rise to all fours. Strength began to surge into his forequarters. There was an urge to push, push upward, raise himself from the ground. As the strength coursed through his body, the urge grew stronger. The colt grunted and struggled and collapsed until within seconds, and almost without realizing how it was done, he was on his legs—legs that stuck out like four ungainly poles, wobbling, unsteady. He, supported by them, was afraid to move.

The mare rubbed her head against the foal's withers, and he collapsed. Soon he was up again, his legs better gathered the second time, though still he staggered and was stiff with uncertainty. After a second tumble, he suddenly understood the idea. The third time that he was up on his legs, he was there to stay. His mother pushed and nibbled and licked at rough patches, but he was strong enough to resist her movements and not be tumbled by them.

Soon he was moving about her, his legs going like

those of a marionette. Within minutes, he was prancing, tossing his large white head, flicking his brushy tail. All stiffness, all strangeness, were gone. He could walk and twist and dance, and his legs were part of him instead of the props they had earlier been.

He sniffed the earth and the grass and the warm body of his dam. She was the only one that attracted him or held meaning for him. The sensitive lips twitched along her body, from breast to flank, from flank to belly. Searching, searching . . . hardly knowing for what they searched, until they discovered the udder with its life-giving milk, hot and rich.

The foal clung excitedly, his whole white body a-quiver, tail flicking, ears twitching, legs stamping. He drank until his belly could hold no more, until he was swollen and uncomfortable. Then the lips relaxed their hold, the pink eyes drooped, and his body slipped into delicious unconsciousness, as he tumbled on the ground beside his mother.

The mare lowered her head and passed her lips across his soft back and swollen flank. Then she began to pull hungrily at the grass, moving in a small circle around the sleeping colt. She seemed unaware of his existence while she grazed. Not once did she lift her head to glance at him or flick an ear in his direction. But not for a moment did her shadow cease to fall very close to him.

II

For the first few days there was little in the colt's life but this sucking at his dam, practicing a gambol or so, and sleeping almost unconsciously. He was still hardly aware of the great herd to which he and his mother belonged. Its members grazed in a scattered fashion. There was not another horse within half a mile of his mother's grazing. He was hardly aware of the rising of the sun or of its setting, so distant was everything from his understanding. He felt the sun's warmth on his back and it pleased him. He felt the playful breeze that tugged at his tail, tickling him and making him dance on his yellow, rubbery hooves. But when the sky grew dark and his mother a dark shadow with it, he did not know that it was because the sun had gone.

For the first few days, his world began and ended with the mother horse. The grass under his hooves, the birds that sang in the grasses by day and screeched blood-curdlingly at night, the sun and the breeze, all were things that held no meaning for him.

On the fourth day of his life, however, various incidents occurred which woke him to the fact that his mother was not the only being in existence besides himself, and that if he used his eyes and his nose and his ears he would grow aware of many things more. It was the day that his mother decided to introduce him to the herd.

On that day, she did not fall to grazing as was her custom but, instead, set off in the direction of her companions. The colt had never seen her move with such determination. He stood staring at her for several minutes, ears pricked, bewildered in expression, as she drew further and further away from him. He bleated after her anxiously and stamped a hoof. The mare halted and looked back, whickering to her youngling, telling him to follow. Then she continued on her way.

The colt was angry now. He stamped again, flattened his ears, and made his first attempt to whinny. The sound came out in a broken squeal and he shook his head in surprise. The mare refused to look back, expecting the colt to obey. He squealed again, stretching out his neck to give more force to the call, and turned angrily from left to right, still stamping and flicking his tail.

The mare stopped, turned her head to stare back at the colt with patient eyes, whinnied once more, and waited. When the colt refused to come, she resumed her walk, ignoring him. The foal lost his righteous anger. His haughty impatience deserted him. He was a baby again, whose mother was far away. He was suddenly afraid. Making up his mind with one last shake of his head, he sprang stiffly into the air, then raced after her. His long white legs swept over the grass gracefully. The breeze grew into a wind as he ran against it, blowing into his eyes and ears and against his neck.

He discovered that there was a joy in running, in feeling the soft turf spring under his hooves. As he neared his dam, his fear disappeared. He began to kick and buck and prance in sheer delight, his pink nostrils stretched wide to breathe in the air that was suddenly nectar. His eyes were bright with joy.

He reached his dam and did not want to stop. He circled around her, racing still, lowering his head between his front legs to buck. The mare hardly glanced at him, used to the ways of foals.

The colt wanted her to notice him. He grew wilder in his game, kicking, tossing, gamboling. Suddenly, his legs knotted themselves over a tuft of thick grass, and he sprawled to the ground with a thud. A breathless bleat of surprise was knocked out of him. For a moment, he lay in a tumbled heap, the sky and the grass swirling about him, making him dizzy. He scrambled up, but he had learned his lesson. When once again his mother called him, he was content to trot along at her side, his muzzle touching her flank, in the sedate manner that all good foals should employ.

They had not gone far when the foal became aware of a new scent assailing his nostrils. His nose twitched and his ears strained eagerly forward. He was aware too of his mother's excitement, and halted when she halted, clinging close to her, almost afraid of this new thing that was happening to him.

There were horses, many horses, none of them far away, and the colt could see as well as smell them. They hardly moved, for most of them were busy grazing. The foal could hear the champing of their jaws and an occasional hoof stamping.

He was startled by the loud neigh suddenly uttered by his mother, and flattened his ears. Simultaneously, most of the horses of the herd stopped their grazing and looked up, ears pricked, in the direction of the mare and the white foal. They stared for a few seconds. One or two whickered a greeting in return, then they dropped their heads again and continued to tear at the grass.

When some seconds had passed, the mare, now sure of her welcome, resumed her walk toward the herd. She had taken no more than a few paces when one of its members broke away from the main bunch and came toward her. It was a yearling colt with gleaming red patches on a white coat. He came toward the lone pair at a fast canter and skidded to a halt just a yard or two away, tossing his head and whickering deep in his throat.

The mare and the yearling stared at each other, the former unperturbed but the yearling very much agitated. He pranced on the spot for a moment or two, then drew closer, hesitatingly, as if unsure of the reception he would be given. The mare tossed her head and slightly changed her direction, moving away from him. The foal, greatly impressed by the newcomer, stood his ground and watched in fascination.

The yearling did not see the foal. He went after the mare, tail swishing, grunting anxiously, trying to push himself under her head. She shied away, nipping at the colt. When he came after her again, she lunged at him in true anger, ripping this time and flattening her ears. The colt squealed, backed away, but again he returned to her, not understanding. This was his mother, at whose side he had run for the whole of a year. That she no longer wanted him was beyond his understanding.

The mare quickly wearied of the importunate animal. All her patience was now for the new foal that followed at her heels. The colt she no longer recognized as her youngling. As he came up to her, cowed and pleading, she thrashed at him with her hooves, buffeting him heavily in the ribs. The colt almost lost his balance as he staggered away. He nearly fell over the albino colt, his brother, and lunged at the slender creature in his anger.

The mother squealed and came after the yearling

again, but the latter knew he was beaten. He dashed back to the herd, aware at last that she had forsaken him. The mare caressed the foal with a movement of her head. She followed the colt, insisting that her youngling stick close beside her.

Soon he and the mare had horses on all sides of them. The foal was afraid of so many of his kind, all towering over him, sniffing at him, nibbling at him before turning away. The mare watched over him carefully to see that none treated him badly in his first contact with them. He cringed against her flank, his eyes big and white-ringed. So many curious muzzles poked at him that his heart beat in fear against his ribs.

His mother seemed on equal terms with all of them and was afraid of none. She pushed away curious yearlings, but welcomed the greetings of her companions. Just as the foal was growing accustomed to the bewildering number of mares that prodded him harmlessly, they all drew aside to make way for the approach of a horse. He was bigger and more powerful than any of them, and they all seemed to be slightly afraid of him. It was the stallion, the lord of the herd, the sire of the albino foal.

He was not the most beautiful of animals. He had dwelt some twenty years on the pampa and had fought many battles. His ears were almost gone, chewed to nothing by his rivals. A great gash scarred all one side of his head, and the eye was withered to a half-closed socket. His whole body was marked with clefts torn by the hooves of his challengers. Only at nightfall, when darkness hid the ugliness, was there a certain beauty in the carriage of his heavily maned head, the haughtiness of his stance, the thickness of his muscles.

He was a gray roan, but twenty winters had whitened the grayness, and now he was almost as white as his albino offspring. The one eye left to him was bold and glittering and wild. The other mares drew away as he approached the albino's dam, snorting, tossing his head, prancing heavily.

She timidly awaited him, accepting the rough caresses he gave her in welcome, hardly moving as he circled about her, sniffing her flanks and back and belly and legs, grunting all the while. The foal was really afraid of this all-powerful being, and backed hurriedly away as, at last, the stallion's attention was drawn to his newest offspring. He drew close to sniff at him.

But it was only cursory attention. His interest was in the mare. He circled about her, ignoring all the others in the herd, while she occasionally returned his attentions and sometimes pulled at the grass.

Grass and Sunshine

The albino foal grew rapidly. He continued to gain his daily sustenance from the mare, and sought her protection whenever there was anything to frighten or disturb him. But a sense of independence drew him gradually further and further from her. The whole of the pampa was his playground, flat, vast, unending. There were many things to discover, many things to see and smell, many things to enjoy.

First, there were the other foals, some older, some younger than himself, all with the same desire to play and explore. By a seemingly common consent, most of the mothers formed a big circle, and the young colts and fillies played within its bounds. They raced about, tossing their heads, their hooves flying. They fought mock battles, the colt foals born with the instinct to bluff with abrupt rearings and stampings. The fillies watched them with curiosity. One day they would watch real stallions fight for possession of them.

When they tired of running and bucking and squealing, they would throw themselves down in twos or threes, keeping the flies from each other with constantly flicking tails. They nibbled at each other's foreheads or necks or withers. Occasionally, they carried on a conversation of short grunts, nickers, and small squeals; or touched noses when they were too hot or too tired for more energetic exchanges.

But the foals were not always in this common nursery. For all that the herd was more or less static, living within the bounds of the grass and herbs that grew abundantly about them, there were times when a general consent to move came over them, and they would march at a grazing pace to new pastures. Then the albino might lose sight of his fellows for several days. The herd moved in a scattered fashion, covering three or four miles from its tip to its tail. Sometimes the albino and his mother would be close to ten or twenty others, and sometimes they were almost completely alone.

The albino would grow impatient with his mother's slow pace, hardly moving two strides in five minutes. He wanted to race and rear and chase the shadows. He would wander off on his own to explore—never very far, always within sight or calling distance of his dam, but far enough for him to feel bold and almost frightened.

It was on these excursions of his own that he grew aware of most of the other pampa dwellers. Following a strange scent that might lead to a thicket of plumy grass, he would come across a nesting bird that would fly up under his nose in fearful surprise, frightening him and sending him cavorting away with snorts and flattened ears. Many birds nested in the grass, but most of them nested in big communities. At the approach of the horses they would rise up with madly flapping wings and screeching voices. The horses would shy away startled, and thus avoid crushing the nests.

On one occasion the albino met an armadillo. The creature attracted him by its strangeness and the unconcerned way it continued its journey, unafraid of the damp, pink nose suddenly prodding at it. It waddled on, perhaps just a little faster as the colt began pushing it with his muzzle. But the albino was not satisfied with just a sniff or so, and suddenly tried pawing at it with his hoof. Then the armadillo decided that it was time to move more rapidly. In spite of its ungainly appearance and former plodding gait, it suddenly shot ahead with astonishing rapidity, downed its nose into the earth, and began a furious digging.

The colt drew closer, ears pricked, eyes bright with interest. Every time he dropped his head to sniff at the strange discovery, the armadillo showered him with earth that sprayed out from its back legs, keeping him at bay. Within seconds, the armadillo was inside the hole that he had dug. Only his tail was visible, and that too, with one last flick, suddenly disappeared. The colt was left with a narrow hole of softly falling earth and a scent that lingered for a few moments to puzzle him.

Another time, the foal spied a group of pampa deer. From a distance they did not seem unlike his playmates. There was no scent, for the breeze was blowing against him. With sudden joy, he set off at a skittish canter toward them. The breeze changed direction, and the albino drew to a startled halt. The scent of the pretty fawn-colored creatures was so repugnant that even curiosity would not draw him closer. He squealed and kicked and shook his head, then turned and galloped back to his dam. He was to meet the harmless deer on many future occasions, but he would never abide the smell of them and would always give them a wide berth.

The spring passed and half the summer. The albino foal and his fellows learned in this time what they might expect to meet and smell and hear on the pampa. They learned to recognize the night noises that had at first startled and even frightened them. The booming of the vizcachas—furry rodents that came up noisily from their burrows when the sun was gone; the squeals and whispers of squabbling, food-hunting rats; the wild screechings and sobbing cries of the different birds were all, by now, a customary harmony without which the foals would probably rest uneasily.

There even came a time when the foal lost interest in his neighbors, so accustomed to them had he grown. The most common of them were the huge rheas and the guanacos that mingled with them. The rheas lived in communities as large as those of the horses. Often the two grazed side by side, keeping apace with each other though never intermingling. The rhea was the cleverest creature on the pampa, cunning, quick-witted, as swift or even swifter than the horses. It would seem that the guanaco sensed this, for he had al-most no sense at all, and was entirely defenseless against any would-be enemy.

The rhea and the guanaco had the same tall necks and haughty, rather silly-looking faces. There was even a similarity in the woolly-looking feathers of the rhea, drooping from his back like gray moss, and the shaggy drooping coat of the guanaco. Both had thickly covered backs and almost naked underparts, both had long legs. One was bird and the other mammal, but they lived in harmony. The guanaco had little need to fear with the rhea to protect him.

II

Until the approach of midsummer, the weather had been benign. The sky was an arc of blue, tossed with clouds as white as the young colt himself. The earth yielded to his tender hooves, ever sprouting grass and flowers to make his soft and sweet-smelling bed. Gradually, the clouds disappeared from the sky. Every day dawned with a heat more intense than its predecessor, The sky was blue, deeply, scorchingly blue. The only thing to break its blueness was the glittering blaze of silver sun, which became unbearable as the day advanced. When such blueness came to the sky, and the sun turned silver in its heat, the grass and the flowers withered and the earth grew hard.

It hurt the colt's hooves to gallop over that summer earth, which was now brown and cracked and moisture-less. The sun that had glowed so pleasantly upon his rump now burned him and seemed to burrow into his very depths, drawing out every drop of energy and leaving him as sapless as the grass. In such heat all the horses stood listless. They had not even the energy to graze, or little appetite for what they found. Their lips swollen with thirst, they pulled at the desiccated grass. When they stamped a hoof to rid themselves of the flies that endlessly bit at their legs, they raised a cloud of fine dust about them.

They passed half the day kicking up dust over their bellies. Some even rolled in it, desperate with the flies that tormented them. The flies were the only beings seemingly unaffected by the racking heat. The foals watched their mothers and followed the set example.

They rolled in the dust, but there was little joy in their rolling. They were as languid as their dams. The heat filled them with inertia; and they stood or lay unmoving, almost like a herd of phantom horses against the shimmering, phantom scenery.

When dusk fell, the earth seemed to stretch a little, released from its long hours of torture. The horses grazed with more animation although the grass they found was tasteless. The foals sucked at their dams with greater eagerness, overcome with appetite in the cool darkness. The mares were not so irritated by them as during the day.

At dusk the herd began to move. It moved of one accord traveling fairly swiftly in comparison with its usual nonchalant gait, for all its members were of one intention. They needed water—water to drink, water to wallow in—the cool contact of mud and rushes.

It took four nights of travel to reach the water nearest to them. As they drew close they could smell it in the air, sweet and tempting. The silent herd grew noisy with restless, anticipatory whickers and grunts. They came upon it just before sunrise, a sullen, marshy river that had shrunk to a trickle surrounded by mud. The trickle continued undaunted until it reached its destination, the mouth of a once wide lake, whose shores were thick with bullrushes, hock-high grass, fragrant herbs, and flowers.

The mares and fillies, the colts, young stallions, and foals, more than eight hundred in all, strung themselves out along the banks of the river and around the lake. They sank up to their bellies in mud and water weeds. They whinnied and tossed their shaggy heads;

they thrashed out and complained. The impatient ones pushed against each other, biting and kicking for a place. It was not long before every horse had bent his head gratefully to the water and sucked slowly with parched lips.

The sun climbed high above them, dispelling the gloom of the night with its golden brightness. As their thirst was satiated some of the herd began to return to the solid banks. They grazed in the grass, still luscious at this place; they chewed the heads off the flowers; they hid themselves in the dark green rushes, and protected themselves from the sun.

Their clumsy retreat flushed wild ducks from their shelter among the rushes. With loud squawks and a great fluster of wings, they glided down to the middle of the lake. Herons and spoonbills stalked with less flurry and more grace across the dried mud flats, delicately paused for a second before continuing through the wet, black mud down to the shrinking water's edge, and dipped their bills to gather up the first moisture of the day. The waders ignored the horses, and the horses seemed unaware of them.

The leader of the herd, the half-blind stallion, was one of the last to desert the water. He had waded into the lake until it almost covered him. He stood there, immobile, soaking his scarred old body in its coolness, the ends of his thick mane touching the water. His favorite mare stood at a little distance from him. The water came up to her hocks, but she would venture no closer to the stallion.

All around the shores of the lake were horses bathing thus. They caked themselves with mud up to their bellies so that the flies could not bite at them.

The albino colt had followed his mother to the water. By the time they had reached it, stirred up by so many bodies and legs, it was murky and hardly appetizing. But the mare drank gratefully, and the colt nibbled at the wavelets. He liked the feel of the cool wetness about him. He waded up to his withers, safe while he could feel the ground beneath his hooves.

When he was still, he could see his reflection in the water. It puzzled him, that other white head with pricked ears and pink, white-whiskered muzzle. When he reached down his nose to sniff at the newcomer, he jumped with surprise as the water flooded his nostrils.

He lost his balance, struggled to regain it, and failed. The water shot up on every side of him; the ducks flew up of one accord with loud shrieks. The stallion in four great bounds was on solid land, his favorite mare beside him. Even the waders held their narrow heads high and looked startled. Meanwhile, the albino foal thrashed about in the water while his dam uttered anxious whinnies from the bank. Then he found land under his hooves again, and raised himself, dripping, from the mire he had stirred up on every side.

Bedraggled and streaked with black mud, the foal staggered to the protection of his dam, snorting and gasping and shaking his waterlogged head. Weeds clung to his ears and legs, and dangled from his tail. He stood on the bank and trembled while his mother nuzzled comfort into him. Then he followed her meekly to a sheltered spot among the rushes, far enough from the water for him to forget his fear of it. He burrowed into the cool green shade of the rushes, and gradually the mud dried over him and clung to his hair. By late afternoon the adventure was forgotten.

He came down to the edge of the lake again, this time not venturing to wet himself. He stood in the soft mud for a long time watching the birds, with pricked ears and bright eyes. The sun shone on the water, making golden ripples in its grayness. The ducks were still squabbling and chasing about noisily.

A sudden shaking of wings drew the colt's attention to the far side of the lake, and there he saw two birds that he had not seen before. White and rose-colored were they, and crimson were the undersides of their wings. It looked as though the sun had caught them in its glow, filling them with the color of sunset. The colt's eyes glimmered with the same color as he stared at the flamingos.

Yearling

The summer passed, and with its passing half of the albino foal's babyhood was gone. He had grown a lot in six months, and was now a sturdy-looking animal. He had thrown off the comical innocence expressed in nearly every movement of his gangling, baby body. His pricked ears, wide-breathing nostrils, and intelligent eyes gave him closer affinity to the future than to the past.

His slender legs were passing gradually from the gamboling, frisky stage and developing a movement that was extravagant in its showiness and gave haughtiness to his stride. He cantered now, rather than frisked. With his long arched neck, proud Roman features, and silky mane and tail, there was a natural beauty about him that many of his companions lacked. He was as strong and long-bodied as they were, but had greater elegance and promise of a greater stature. In all, he gave signs that he was a throwback to the Jennets, with their oriental blood, whom the Spaniards first brought to the land. It was blood which still coursed strongly through all the criollo ponies, although its dominant features were mainly lost through the natural selection forced upon them in their unhampered wanderings.

In the herd to which the albino belonged, there were perhaps fifty horses as beautiful as he was destined to become, among them grays with black points, bays, and most of the roans. There was a nobility in their expression, in the carriage of their heads, and their graceful movements that all their wildness could never deny. The albino possessed this same nobility and, as his foalhood gradually faded, it began to show.

With the coming of autumn, began the best time of all for the colt. The molesting summer heat was gone, and there were showers which refreshed both animals and plants alike. The ground grew soft and resilient again, perfect for prancing over, and began to sprout the first green blades of winter grass at which the horses tugged with so much eagerness.

The colt, too, was tempted to browse among such tender shoots, and their sweetness soon had him pulling and searching with as much voraciousness as his mother. He still came to her for the bulk of his sustenance, but she began to push him aside with greater impatience, swinging her hindquarters in his path or crossly kicking whenever his head came searching under her belly. After a while, the colt decided that the grass was as sweet as milk to him, and no longer demanded as insistently as he had in foalhood.

At first, he was often hungry, and lost some of his tubbiness. He had to roam for his food, and had less time to gambol and play. His dam had no scruples about snatching the most luscious patches from him, so he found it wiser to graze apart from her.

Little by little his independence grew. He still followed her when the herd was on the move; he still drew close to her at dusk to spend the night beside her. But during the day, their paths hardly crossed even though they were within calling distance.

The colt was gregarious by nature and had no desire to be alone. He struck up a friendship with another colt about his own age, a bay with a twisted white blaze. They were always together. They grazed side by side, their muzzles often touching as they searched after the same sweet grass. When they were not grazing, they would stand head to tail, swishing the flies from each other's unprotected flank. They fought mock battles, rearing, nipping, squealing. Engrossed in each other's company, they hardly noticed the existence of their earlier playmates.

II

The winter passed as uneventfully as the summer. Except that the grass shot up ever more abundantly, so that the horses grew fat and hardly moved, the foal discovered that the weather was not so friendly as in the summer. It gradually grew colder and colder. Even though the hair on his body grew thicker and fat began to form under his skin, there were many mornings that began in miserable shiverings, and nights when the frost was so thick that his breath hung frozen on the air. The grass also froze and lost its sweetness, and the ground grew hard again, as in summer.

Before the frost, there were many weeks of almost incessant rain, when the earth was covered with lakes and churned with mud. Winter birds settled on the lakes and were in their element, while the horses stared miserably at the flooded meadows and chewed at the soggy fodder with little appetite. In the summer it was pleasant to be covered with mud so that the flies could not bite, but in the winter the mud was clammy and never dried, and the horses were cold and uncomfortable. They had no protection against the downpours from the sky, and stood with drooping heads while the heavy rain bounced off their backs and poured down their flanks. The sun had deserted them, and the sky was always white and gray-streaked with clouds.

But winter did not last forever. Gradually the skies began to clear again, the sun to shine more lingeringly, the showers to become less frequent. The birds that had fled the pampa during its coldness began to return. The days were filled with the noise of them, as in great colonies they squabbled and searched for old nests or fought over new ones. The sheets of rainwater shrank and began to disappear. Occasionally, there were days when the sun was really hot, and vapor rose from the earth to hang in clouds above the grass.

The horses began to cast their shaggy winter coats, and most of them looked unkempt, dirty, and ragged. The albino was no exception. He was almost a yearling now and no longer sucked his mother's milk. His fatness was a grass fatness, and though there were strong muscles beneath his skin they hardly showed for the plumpness the heavy winter grazing had given him.

But with the change in the weather and the skylarks and lapwings soaring in the sky or drumming in the grass, the colts and fillies grew skittish again. The bright sun put spring in their hooves and, although all winter they had almost forgotten how to play, they suddenly remembered again. Throughout the whole herd, the youngsters began to frisk and gambol and toss their heads, throwing off the sluggishness of winter.

The albino and the bay with the crooked blaze took to racing each other across the flat grasslands. They raced with a grace that was beautiful to behold, as free as the swans that flew over their heads, their long legs outstretched, almost floating over the grass in their joy; their heads high, eyes brilliant with delight; tails and manes and forelocks combed out behind them by the wind. Sometimes the albino would draw ahead, sometimes the bay; sometimes they would swirl in midflight to prance and rear and snort in pretended rage, feeling for the first time the stallion blood that was in them. They pawed at each other, but with careful hooves. They circled and whickered and walked on their hind legs. Then of one accord they would break into a gallop again, and one would chase the other, snapping at the rump in front.

Such was the surging of springtime in their blood that they hardly thought of grazing, or even felt hunger. They would snatch a few mouthfuls of grass or thistles, then buck and toss and swirl about. Sometimes the two of them would pound wildly through the center of a bunch of staidly grazing matrons, or, with the impatience of their flying hooves, send a colony of peewits into scandalous outcry.

Mostly they raced, on and on and on, using up their eternal energy, circling the herd at such a distance that in the whole day they would hardly see a member of it. They were always in each other's company and returned only to their dams at nightfall, when their brazen courage would desert them, frightened away by the haunting cries of the widow birds or the scent of a lion in the grass.

Then they would fall to grazing seriously, weary of running and playing, ravenously hungry. The albino, a foal again, would cling to his dam and rub himself against her, seeking her caresses. Somewhere among the shadows of dark bodies the bay would be doing the same.

III

The vizcachas dug long, deep, and complicated tunnels beneath the pampa grass, throwing out the earth behind them in huge mounds. Somewhere under these mounds, in darkness and secrecy and freedom from danger, the young of the vizcachas were born and nursed. The big rheas made themselves an untidy nest in the middle of a bunch of giant thistles, wild artichokes, or plumy pampa grass. They laid big eggs from which eventually hatched the baby rheas, from birth as wily and as swift as their parents. The skylarks nested in tussocks of grass; the wild duck among the canebrakes and amid the rushes along the edges of a water course.

The deer and the guanaco dropped their young in a secluded place, and within an hour the babies were running at their heels, the guanacos as white and woolly as the spring clouds. The rats, the armadillos, the snakes, each found a place in which to bring forth their young. Even the fearsome lion nested somewhere on the pampa. The horses were like the deer and the guanaco and the wild cattle they occasionally encountered. They drew away from the herd to a private place, returning only when the youngling could follow and more or less defend itself.

Thus it was that one day, when the albino returned from his games and his races with the bay colt, he looked in vain for his mother. He went from group to group in search of her, stopping to snatch a few mouthfuls of grass every now and then, not really perturbed, for his need of her was automatic rather than essential. But as each mare turned her back on him or shouldered him away, not wanting him near her, a certain anxiety began to niggle at him, born of custom and a fear of loneliness.

His search grew more determined, and he forgot the grass that had before distracted him. He came across the bay colt, grazing just a few yards from his dam. The albino whinnied, and his companion looked up with pricked ears but was not tempted to follow him. Night was coming on. The individual outlines of the horses were fading into one long irregular shadow. Lions prowled in the grass at night, and a colt was wise who stayed with his mother.

For a while the albino stopped beside the bay, grazing with him. Every few seconds he raised his head and looked about him anxiously. But seeing that his companion cared nothing for his plight, he eventually went away and continued his search.

For most of the night the albino colt looked for his mother and called to her in vain. He gained a few nips and kicks from the other mares whom he startled in the darkness, but sympathy from none. Never had he noticed before how dark and how long was the night. He was afraid to lie down, having no mother to watch over him; and he was afraid to be alone. But there was no other mare that wanted him near. He wandered disconsolately from group to group, standing for a while at a short distance from them, trying to find comfort just in the presence of the other mothers, hoping perhaps that one of them would accept him.

Little by little his head drooped and his weary legs tired of constant movement. Each halt became more prolonged until in the end, overcome by misery and weariness, he found himself a spot alone from which he could at least see the rest of the herd and gain some comfort. There, with the moon glistening upon his white flanks, he fell asleep.

The next day he played as usual with the bay colt, and while he was racing and cavorting in the sunshine he forgot his loneliness and outcast state. It was only at dusk that he again remembered, and for a second time began the fruitless search for the mother he had inexplicably lost. The second night he passed as he had done the first, lingering long in the company of the bay colt but unable to dispel the desolation that crept over him with the deepening of the darkness and the wild cries of the animals that lived on the fringes of the horse community.

The third night, too, was the same for him, looking for his dam and feeling fear and loneliness without her.

Now he was afraid to leave the herd. He sensed somehow that she must return and he wanted to be there waiting for her. He was impatient of the bay's efforts to draw him away and played only halfheartedly before breaking off and circling back to the herd. The colt followed, teasing and coaxing with many head tossings, pawings, and whickerings. But the albino knew that his mother would come, and he spent the best part of the morning pacing with that high, showy gait of his, back and forth, back and forth.

The bay colt tired and went away. Later he came back, and still the albino kept the vigil for his mother. His companion joined him, and for a while they cropped the grass, side by side, noses touching, lifting their heads simultaneously every now and then to watch the horizon, both beautiful in their alert youthfulness.

Suddenly, the albino's instinct was rewarded. Before the afternoon was far advanced he saw his mother jogging toward him—at least he thought she was coming toward him. But he noticed how she stopped every now and then to look back and seemed not to care at all that he was waiting for her. Filled with joy, he called shrilly to her. She made no answer and seemed to be unaware of his existence.

He threw himself at a gallop to meet her but drew to a halt before he was close enough to touch her. At her heels tottered a lank brown foal, walking with uncertainty. It was this odd creature that held all the mare's attention. The albino felt hostility in her, and because of this he hesitated.

This was his mother and yet she was his dam no longer. This was what he smelled in her, and it bewildered him exceedingly. The brown foal meant nothing to him. He could not connect it with his dam. He took no heed of his mother's warning actions, and drew close, as always, to be caressed by her.

He was too close to avoid the teeth that suddenly tore at him, and drew back with a squeal of pain, a patch of blood rapidly staining his pure white flank. This was no admonishing nip that held a caress, even while it punished. The colt was halted in his tracks, utterly disconcerted. Again his mother ignored him, interested only in the foal. But when the albino warily tried to follow beside her, she assaulted him a second time and drove him off with whirlwind fury, teeth and hooves and squealing rage.

The albino fled, ears flattened and eyes wild with fear. He had no memory of a time when, like the brown foal, he came innocently at the heels of his dam, to dispossess a brother as now he was dispossessed.

For several days he lingered near his mother, unable to believe that not only did she no longer want him, but would actually attack him if he drew too close. His cloud-white hide was bruised by her hooves and teeth. Engrossed by his dam's strange behavior and the foal that clung to her flank and eyed him with fear, he almost forgot the existence of the bay colt. But when at last he realized that his mother would never revoke her rejection of him, he tired of hanging around her and once again went in search of the other colt.

He found the bay deserted like himself. His dam, too, had another youngling tottering at her heels. They rubbed noses and exchanged greetings. Then, with one accord, they broke into a wild, head-tossing gallop, and fled from the herd as if lions were after them. The thunder of their hooves startled the placidly grazing mares, and caused even the stallion to lift his head and watch them for a moment, wondering at their excitement.

Pampa Fire

*Several years went by. The colts grew and became stal-*lions. They still followed the herd, part of it and yet apart. Both had developed into magnificent animals, proud with youth and strength. Their long solid bodies rippled with muscles, and the sun on their backs made the gloss of their coats seem even brighter. The albino especially was beautiful, with a heavy mane that cascaded to his withers, a thick forelock that almost hid his eyes, and a bannerlike tail that swept through the grasses.

The two animals played less often now, though they continued to graze amicably in each other's company, nose to tail, swishing the flies from each other's flanks and withers. When they played, their mock battles were inclined to become real ones, for neither was as placid as their still figures would suggest. An accidental blow with a hoof would cause the stallion tempers to boil. The pricked ears would flatten, teeth were bared, and a clash was inevitable if one or the other was disinclined to submit.

With the leader of the herd, they were afraid to battle. The old one-eyed stallion still held full sway over his mares, and any of his sons that tried to steal them from him soon regretted it. He was implacable in his rage. No one blow or two would satisfy him. He would chase his usurpers across the pampa for miles, forcing them into self-defense and battering them with his hard, experienced hooves and teeth until they bowed their heads in total submission.

Both the bay and the albino, young stallions still, respected him too much to try to steal his mares. They would haze around them when they could, and exchange a few grunts and caresses. But the mares grew noisy and excited in the presence of another stallion, so that soon the old one would grow aware of the situation and be down upon the thieves with a squeal of fury that was usually enough to frighten them away. His sons would retire to a safe distance, watching the mares and impatiently stamping, sometimes shaking their heads in anger at the old stallion, but not daring to accept his challenge or to go closer while he was watching.

Neither one of them ever thought of leaving the herd and going his own way in search of mares for himself. The pampa was wide and lonely for a solitary animal, with not even a tree to shade him from the sun and, perhaps, a lion lurking behind every tuft of grass. The sight, smell, or even sound of the big herd was a necessary comfort to the two animals that otherwise grazed alone. They had been born within its radius, and it was as much a part of their existence as the sky and the earth and the revolving seasons.

II

It was during the albino stallion's sixth summer that the first real danger came to threaten him. It came in an insidious fashion, a scent in the breeze that caused him to wrinkle his pink nostrils for a moment and raise his head as he sought to recognize it. Then the breath of danger disappeared before the albino could puzzle over it. He began to graze again, the thing forgotten.

The sun was hot that day, perhaps the hottest of all that long and weary summer. Only the changeable breeze made the heat bearable. The two stallions sought spasmodically among the withered grass and flowers for something worth eating. Now and again one or the other would lift his head and widen his nostrils, scenting again the puzzling odor that came with the wind. By nightfall, the heat had not abated and all the horses of the herd were restless. The strange scent was stronger now, and because they could not recognize it they were disturbed.

The old stallion wheeled constantly about his herd, grunting and whistling through his nostrils, pushing the struggling mares into some semblance of solidity. Fear was growing within him, perhaps instinctive, perhaps remembered, and this it was that made him bunch his big herd together, mares and fillies, and the foals that followed them. He snapped and struck at the yearling colts that attempted to cling too closely to the herd. They were no longer his responsibility— in fact, they were his future enemies. In times of threatened danger tolerance was forgotten.

But the night passed uneventfully. A clear half-moon cast a gloomy light over the dry grasslands and nervous horses. The breeze continued to carry the insidious warning, recognized by the horses but not understood.

The sun came to the sky in a mist of orange light,

and as the morning progressed the sky grew yellow instead of blue. Now the scent was much stronger on the breeze that bowled playfully toward the herd, and a noise was growing among its members as mares whickered nervously or whinnied to their younglings.

The breeze was heavy with the acrid smell of burnt cane, thistle, and dried grass. As the day progressed and the sky lowered over them, there was no freshness left in the breeze at all. Its gusts came thick with smoke, and the horizon was blurred as if with fog.

Slowly, still not fully aware of the danger that threatened them, the herd began to move with the breeze; the satellite animals, like the albino and the bay, followed. The sky grew dark. The horses began to snort and neigh as the clean air was swallowed up relentlessly minute by minute. A flock of rheas came running alongside the horses, covering the pampa in huge, effortless strides. Soon the rheas were far ahead, a straggling herd of guanacos behind them. The horses caught their alarm and began to move faster.

But a jogging, bewildered mass of animals cannot move as swiftly as an unfettered wind. Soon the horizon was broken with streaks of light among the grayness, flickering low at first, then shooting into lively, dancing sheets of brightness. The pampa was on fire.

How quickly those giddy tongues of fire traveled, borne by a breeze that knew no halting. For three days it had burned. Its rapacious hunger was increased by what it fed on: a thirsty pampa, thick with dry thistle and bracken, carpeted with wilted grass and flowers. The vizcachas and the armadillos were suffocated in their holes, the ground birds roasted in their nests. The rheas, the guanacos, and the horses fled until their eyes bulged and their hearts burst and the flames overtook them.

The fire was as fickle as the breeze that bore it, turning first this way and then another, devouring creatures that had the day before escaped and now lay panting and at rest, believing themselves to be free of danger.

The scorching heat reached the horses long before the flames. Those that came behind grew wild with fear, and pushed against the rumps in front of them, fighting for a passageway through them. The jogging gait had grown into a canter, the canter to a gallop, and, as the horizon burst into flame, the whole herd of some eight hundred animals was thundering across the still free grassland ahead of them, necks stretched out, tails streaming.

They ran blindly, fear their master. There was no mare mother enough to desert the dash for safety to heed a youngling left behind, bawling terror and desolation. The herd streamed out into a long, thick line, the swift to the fore, the old, the lame, the weary bringing up the rear. The one-eyed stallion led them. But ahead of him, though at a wide distance, raced his two throwback sons, the albino and the bay.

Birds flew up under the stampeding hooves, to be crushed and left to the flames that followed. A herd of deer bounded alongside the horses, and for once the latter were unaware of them. There were only two smells on the pampa now, one of fear, the other of fire.

All day the fire followed the herd. Little tongues of flame, licking over the dry grass in streams, were followed by cascades of smoke and fire. Other times the fire was held back by the changing wind, seemingly straining against the force that tethered it and searching to east and west for outlet. Lone animals were left behind in the smoke, exhausted or lamed, shadows until the fire took them. And the big herd of eight hundred had become scattered bunches of fleeing horses, no longer united, each one living in his own world of terror and oblivious of the rest.

The old stallion still kept well to the fore, as well as most of the younger animals. Of them all, the albino and his companion were at the best advantage. They had left the herd behind long since, unhampered from the beginning. These two raced side by side as they often had raced in fun. Now, their eyes bulged with strain, their mouths sawed at the dry air, breath rasped in their throats, and their glossy coats were dirty with sweat and the smoke of the fire, which coated them with grayness.

By nightfall, they had gained enough on their relentless pursuer to pause for rest. But it was an alert, uneasy rest, and they neither thought of grazing nor felt hunger. Both were desperately thirsty. The air was dry with the heat of the fire and thick with ash which floated in the breeze. But in this place there was no water. Even the breeze was hot and tickled their wide-stretched nostrils, offering them no alleviation. The two young stallions did not rest for long. Terror was still their companion.

Long before the darkness of the night was broken, they were off at a canter again. The sound of their hooves was loud over the unusually silent pampa. On and on the two stallions fled, the bay's eyes as red as the albino's. Now and again they mingled with the rheas and guanacos or with other horses, but they shied away from numbers and ran faster alone.

Southward they traveled. Some two hours after they had left their resting place, the flames had reached it. They did not halt as had done the stallions, but continued their swirling, devouring dance. The night sky glowed redly as it reflected the fire that refused to die. Between the two stallions and the fire was only the empty pampa. The rest of the herd was lost somewhere, perhaps overtaken by the flames. Even its wily, one-eyed leader did not come prancing and blowing—nor would he again.

The stallions came eventually to a river, wide and slow and marshy, its level much sunken because of the summer heat that had sucked its moisture, and into this they gratefully plunged. The water caressed their exhausted bodies. They stood up to their bellies in it for an hour or more, drinking avidly until their thirst was satiated. Then, more slowly, they struggled through its depths and came to shore on a muddy bank where ducks sunned themselves and a few herons dozed on one leg, unaware of the fire that raged at so little a distance from them.

The horses were affected by the tranquillity of the place and made another halt, snatching at the grass that still grew greenly along the bank. The fire reached the horizon and the stallions snorted, shook their heads, and trembled. They wheeled away from the river and startled the ducks with the terror-struck sound of their hooves.

The fire reached the river and there at last it was

halted. The breeze was tired of playing with the flames and deserted them on the bank instead of blowing them across. The river was too wide to be leaped by even the most avid of fires, and for several hours it swept up and down the long, long bank of the river, searching, devouring, tiring, dying.

The water birds had fled to its other bank and, crouched among the cool rushes, watched the monster gradually die, leaving a scorched, blackened shadow of itself over all the pampa. For days afterward smoke rose up from the earth, thin and gray, and the ducks could not return to their side of the river without burning themselves.

Miles to the south, the two stallions halted. The breeze was no longer heavy with burning. Instead it blew sweetly fresh from the colder, southern lands. They came back to the river in search of water and fresh grazing. They could not return to their old grazing grounds, for there was nothing left but the smell of terror and the smoke that continued to spiral upward.

Gauchos

The pampa that had always seemed so free from danger now began to show its other nature to the two stallions: first, in the all-destructive fire of which they were reminded for a long time because of the acrid smell that was blown to them whenever the wind came from across the burned-out grasslands; secondly, in another more violent manner, when for the first time in their six summers of life, they were pursued and captured by the only creature on the pampa they had not known of, man.

They had grazed beside the rheas and the guanacos all their lives. They had slept at night with the voices of the vizcachas booming in their ears, and the scratchings and whisperings of other rodents a comforting accompaniment. They knew all the birds, both large and small; they had even gone stiff with fright at the rank smell of lion which lingered in some brackeny spot where a puma had nested. Of this other creature who rode upon the backs of their own kind, made slaves of them, and was greater in wile, persistence, and cruelty than all of their enemies, they knew nothing.

Their first awareness of man's existence came one early morning when they were grazing beside the same river that had previously saved their lives. The sky was still dark in the west, and the moon shone palely. Over the water hung a lacy mist, which clung to the webs spun by spiders among the rushes. It was a time of silence on the pampa, when the night animals had returned to their underground holes, the night birds to their nests, and the day creatures had not yet ventured from sleeping.

The two stallions stood at the water's edge, quenching their thirst unhurriedly. The albino was hardly more than a shadow in the milk-colored mist. He lifted his head, ears pricked, having caught the faintest of sounds in those silent moments. The bay soon followed his example, and the two stood alert and listening. The sound was of their own kind, that of galloping hooves. The sound came from the other side of the river, across the fire-scorched earth. The stallions quivered with anticipation as they listened. Since the fire, they had neither seen nor heard any of their own kind.

As they listened and waited, the sun broke through the mist. Darkness fled, though the moon lingered some minutes longer, and the stallions caught sight of those traveling so swiftly toward them.

It was a troop of about three dozen horses. The stallions watched with interest, sensing no danger, though the galloping hooves filled them with restlessness and set their own hooves dancing over the soft soil beside the river. They wheeled about, and whickered and snorted. They eventually became aware of the strange, almost birdlike creatures the two leading horses carried on their backs. In their innocence they were unfraid.

And so they waited until the gauchos were close

enough to frighten them with their loud shrieks, their cracking whips, the roughness of their movements, the total strangeness of their appearance and smell. Then the two stallions fled. The calm of the morning was broken by loud turbulent splashes as the gauchos forded the river in pursuit of the two beautiful animals, and by their triumphant shouts of laughter as they urged on their mounts and whirled the bolas about their heads.

The bay let out a squeal as he crashed to the ground. A second later the albino also was flung to the earth, his hind legs entangled by the stones and leather which had wound themselves around him in half-a-dozen twirls. He screamed with surprise and fear, lashed out with all four legs, and rolled and twisted on the ground. But the thongs only tightened themselves about him, increasing his fear and rage.

He made several vain efforts to rise to all fours, and for a moment stood clumsily before plunging himself off balance again. Then the horses and their gaucho riders were upon him, and he became their captive.

A lasso was put around his neck, in spite of his plunging hooves and head. With the same length of cord, they tied up his off-foreleg and pulled up the knee to the level of his chin, so that although he could stand he could not move, as he learned after several clumsy falls. Thus they left him while they went to remove the bolas from the bay and halter him in a similar fashion.

Then they went back across the river to hobble their bell mares and assure that their horses did not stray. They were deaf to the distressed cries of the two captive stallions, plunging and falling and vainly fighting the cords that held them. The gauchos were as thrilled as children with a new toy, exclaiming over the beauty of the two animals and the fun they would have trying to ride them.

The sky was blue now and the moon had vanished. The mist no longer hung over the river or clung to the cobwebs in the rushes. The water birds did not come out of their sleeping places, frightened by the cries and snorts of the two stallions, and the sound of the men who had come to disturb the tranquillity of the pampa.

II

On those wide and empty grasslands, only half explored, and whose soil was still mostly unbroken by the tools of man, compassion, gentleness, and understanding were unknown qualities. The horses knew nothing of them and neither did the men. They were two brute forces, competing, one against the other. The horses had the greater strength, the men the greater cunning and cruelty. The horses expected to suffer at the hands of their captors, and for this they feared them greatly; and the men would inflict suffering upon them, for it was the only kind of strength they knew. They laughed and joked with each other as the stallions trembled and the birds stayed hidden in the rushes. They advanced upon their captives.

With the swiftness of the armadillo when it digs itself a hole, they released the two stallions from their crippling postures and were upon their backs. The reaction of the bay and albino was simultaneous. Both squealed with fear and rage, and reared, their front legs savagely pawing the air. The gauchos yelled and beat at them with their whips. The horses forgot the existence of each other, so engrossed were they in their own private battle.

The cries of the men and horses mingled and echoed across the pampa. Dust flew up from the dry ground, making their eyes smart. The albino twisted and reared and bucked and tried in every possible way to throw the creature that clung to his back, raking him with huge, three-pointed spurs, and thrashing his head and rump with the whip. The bay did likewise. At times they were close together, but not seeing each other; at times they were far apart. The two horses that watched them rolled their eyes and tugged against the reins that restrained them, sharing the fear of their wild brothers, perhaps remembering their own initiation into the ways of the gauchos.

Never had the albino felt such hot anger and terror, and the two combined made him ignore all weariness and pain. Though his heart pounded with giddying force, though his legs trembled and threatened to forsake him, though his mouth and nostrils were choked with dust and froth, and his flanks were raw and bloody where the spurs punished him, he would recognize no end to the battle until the monstrous thing that clung to him was beneath his hooves and vanquished.

Squeals of anger became squeals of desperation. When he could no longer voice his terror loudly, he grunted and snorted and tossed even more wildly. But the man on his back was impervious to all his raging, and as tireless as the horse was exhausted. There seemed to be no way of dislodging him until, suddenly, the bay stallion collapsed. For no more than half a second was the attention of the albino's rider diverted, but it was all that the desperate horse was looking for.

He nearly dislocated his back with the last desperate lunge that he gave, his legs stiff, his chin almost touching his belly. A wild cry of triumph escaped him as he felt the gaucho slipping. One more toss and he was free. The gaucho was stumbling on the ground beside him. Before he could regain his balance and grab the halter, the albino was away, racing as he had never raced in all his life.

Free of the gaucho, his frenzy subsided. His long legs swept over the dry pampa with the ease of a bird caught in the wind. He galloped with his head held high and proudly, and when he finally halted he was a long way from the scene of the battle. His whole body trembled with weariness. Only now did he begin to feel the stinging cuts slashed in his flanks by the spurs, only now did he realize that the halter was still about his head, its rope trailing along the ground. Now, also, did he realize that he was alone. The bay stallion had not followed him.

For all his weariness, the albino could not rest. He kept circling about, uttering short whinnies and grunts, pawing at the ground. Now and again, he shook his head impatiently or tried to rub off the halter against a front leg. Often he looked in the direction from which he had come, scenting the river water in the wind and the faint smell of burning, which still hung over the pampa. But the bay stallion did not come, nor even the scent of him, and the albino whickered softly to himself, disconsolate.

He grazed for a while, snatching at a few unpalatable patches of grass. The sharp cry of a bird startled him, and he set off at a gallop as if pursued again. The rope jerking along beside him added to his terror, and he fled from it in vain.

For the best part of the day he kept on running, frightened by the slightest sound or movement. When night came, and with it the usual nocturnal sounds and activities, his fear faded. He had learned to interpret the sounds of the rodents and knew by listening to them that they were tranquil. At last, he stopped running away.

The moon illuminated his solitary whiteness on the lonely plain. He stood with drooping body, dozing. Now and again, he roused himself to rub at the halter, and with wakefulness he would realize that he was alone. Three times in the night he called to the bay with loud echoing neighs that startled the vizcachas. The only answer that came back to him was the unchanging sounds of the pampa night.

The gauchos had taken his companion. The albino felt as lonely as a motherless foal, for never had he grazed without the bay somewhere near. Often he would look up from eating, with pricked ears, wondering for a moment where the other was. Then he would remember. When he cantered or galloped, the sound of his hooves was a lonely one. It was no longer echoed by those of the bay.

Hatred grew in the heart of the albino, the first he had ever experienced. It was a hatred particularly intense, for at the same time he was afraid. The bay had been his shadow for a lifetime. Now all that he had was the memory of the gauchos' violence and their rope around his head.

Terror

All that summer and the following winter the white stallion remained alone. His solitary state lay heavily upon him. He had never lived without the sound and smell of the herd, nor without the presence of the bay. His unanswered neighs and whinnies filled him with a sense of loneliness. He managed to rid himself of the rope that had irritated him; his scarred flanks healed and were hidden by the hair that grew thickly over them. The memory of that violent morning faded, but his loneliness grew greater.

At the coming of spring, when the peewits and plover were preening themselves and courting, and all the birds were busy with nest-making; when the larks flooded the early mornings with music and the fleecy young of the guanacos were gamboling in the new grass, the albino knew that he could dwell alone no longer. Instinct impelled him to search out his own kind. He wandered for many days, tearing at the new grass as he went, smelling and listening and calling.

He was beautiful in his eagerness, his white head proudly held, his high, free gait a princely movement, his coat as pure as swan's down. He was as free as the birds, and the pampa he trod over was his own. The blood within him thrilled at the pure joy of being alive, at the wind in his nostrils and the sun on his back and the never-ending plains to race over.

He ran with the joy of bird in flight. At times, he was hardly more than a colt in his enthusiasm, bucking, snorting, pretending fear at his own shadow or the rustle of the wind through the thistles. When, at last, there was the smell of horses in the air, the scent of other stallions, his playfulness fell away.

Arrogance overcame prudence. He swept about the herd with an airy gallop, calling to the mares, challenging the colts and stallions. All was confusion among them at the sight and sound of this fearless intruder.

Tranquillity was lost among the excited, whickering mares. The colts felt his challenge but shrank from answering it. Only one voice echoed in answer to the albino's, that of the small herd's master. He came from among the mass of horses, slowly but unafraid, walking on his hind legs and pounding the ground with his front hooves, his throat full of angry whistlings.

Hardly any older than the albino, he was a strong, good-looking stallion, mealy colored, his vision half lost behind an unchecked forelock, his small ears already champed in another battle. The albino ignored him and swept once more about the herd as if to show the other horse that from this day onward it would be his. Its master squealed a second warning, flinging into it a righteous challenge.

The albino checked his course. The smell of the herd excited him and filled his whole being with the determination to possess it. He advanced upon the black-maned lord who crashed angry hooves to the ground, whistling his own imperious anger.

The mares drew back in timid fear as the two male animals suddenly engaged in combat. The albino attacked with the fury of a usurper determined to win;

the other defended his right with equal rage. There were the sounds of hooves striking flesh, of teeth that clashed as they sought each other's throats. Not for a moment did they stand off and rest, for both were young and rage-filled, and the heat of their blood made them heedless of wounds. There was no bluff, no caution, no quarter yielded. They tore at each other with all their savage stallion anger until one would give way or be crushed.

The mealy colored stallion was smaller than his adversary, and eventually the difference began to tell. Both were torn and bloody in many places. It was not until the albino brought down a hoof that landed sharply on the other's skull that the battle ended. The smaller horse staggered with the blow, and his legs doubled under him. The albino renewed his attack as the other quavered, and might have killed him had not the other found the last-minute strength that kept him from sprawling. Instead, he dragged himself away from the albino's reach, all his proud anger gone. His blood-matted head drooped, and the white stallion knew that he was vanquished.

The albino advanced threateningly. The other stallion backed a few paces more, offering no defense except in admitting his defeat. The albino was satisfied, but he continued to chivy his adversary until, at last, he was at a good distance from the herd that had been his, outcast forever.

The albino returned to his newly won mares, who had gone back to grazing, uninterested in the fate of their former lord. In turn they crowded about him. There was much whickering and squealing as they smelled at him and accepted him. In these first moments of possession and glory, the stallion took no heed of the gashes in his neck and withers and flanks, cleft by the other's hooves, around which the flies were already buzzing. He accepted the mare's caresses and offered some of his own. When this was done, he sought out the colts and gave them a taste of his heels and teeth so that they should learn to respect him.

In the afternoon, he fought two minor battles with a couple of younger stallions who had for the past year been kept in check by the strength of the vanquished master. Both he cast out from the herd, permitting them no quarter, for they would be his enemies always.

By nightfall, he was overcome with weariness and his wounds were beginning to ache. But he moved among his newly acquired mares, proud and contented, sniffing at one, nipping another. In the distance, the young, outcast stallions watched him rancorously. The albino was aware of them but untroubled. For the moment, at least, he was king.

II

More than a year went by. The albino stallion lived in tranquillity with his mares. The herd numbered just over a hundred, including the young colts and the foals. It was a small one in comparison with the one that the albino had previously known. He was quite content, however, for all of them were his. He had no memory now of that other herd, with its fearful one-eyed stallion. Neither did he remember the bay colt, nor even the fire. The only thing that stayed in his memory was his fear of man. This remained, because more than once in that year did he see an occasional horse and rider.

The slightest glimpse was all he needed to feel again the rage and desperation that had once filled him. It was almost as if he could still feel the gaucho on his back and his shouts in his ears. With shaking head, he would prance and snort, then gather up his mares and lead them to a safer place.

The stallion did not know that there were various small ranches on that side of the river, and even a hamlet beyond the horizon. Cattle and sheep grazed over that part of the pampa. When the stallion sometimes spied them from a distance, he would draw hurriedly away, for with them came the smell of man. He kept the mares almost endlessly on the move until he was satisfied that there was no danger.

But the albino had no knowledge of the ways of man, only of other animals like himself that would not molest him if he left them alone. His instinct told him that if he moved away, the men would not touch him. So he kept on moving erratically southward, feeling safe in this way. He could not know that men might covet him for his beauty, or his mares for their skins and their heavy tails. Leaving him in peace now was not a promise that they would never molest him.

So it was that on a warm morning, halfway between spring and summer, when the albino felt himself safe and the memory of man had almost faded, he heard again the wild shrieks that had set his heart pounding. He saw in the distance a number of gauchos traveling toward him. His reaction was as it had been that other time. He fled, giving no thought to the mares that were his pride. They, seeing his fear and hearing the far-off noises, grew agitated and fearful also.

Within minutes, all were copying his example. The

tranquil day thundered with the sound of their hooves. Birds flushed in fright and flapped over the backs of the stampeding horses. A herd of deer caught the fear and, with grass still between their jaws, leaped alongside them.

They fled toward the unhampered east, but suddenly there were gauchos in that direction too. The stallion, seeing them first, reared and swerved toward the south. Here were still more men and horses, and these were followed by dogs that yammered their bloodlust. The albino changed direction, racing hither and thither. Wherever he went, he encountered more gauchos.

The mares, confused and terrified, scattered in every direction. They collided into each other, dashing about like ants on an upset anthill. Around them galloped the stallion, neighing shrilly, as terrified and as confused as they.

The gauchos closed in on them. The sound of the bolas, swirling above their heads, was like the rushing of a winter wind. The deadly weapons left their owners' hands, and within seconds horses were beginning to stagger and fall. Once they were down, there was no getting up. As they struggled to all fours, the gaucho to whom the bolas belonged would be upon his prey. One spring from the saddle, one slash with his knife, and the horse would be either hamstrung or pulsing out its life from a severed jugular vein. Then the gaucho was up again, the bolas swinging once more, to chase after another vainly fleeing mare.

There were some thirty men and a hundred horses. The hunt spread across a distance of four or five miles, miles that became littered with gasping, fallen bodies, as one by one the free ones were pulled down. When there remained but three or four horses, the gauchos suddenly became aware of the stallion that led them, racing like a cloud with the wind behind it, beautiful in his wild frenzy.

"For me!" cried one, standing up in the stirrups to broadcast his claim.

"For me!" cried the rest simultaneously, and the dead and dying horses they had left behind them were suddenly forgotten as they set out upon this new chase, each intent to have the fabulous stallion for himself.

But their mounts were already tired and beginning to flag in spite of the excited spurs that tore at them mercilessly. The albino had never galloped so swiftly or been so afraid. He left the few remaining mares behind. With eyes bulging and heart bursting, he flung himself headlong in the only direction left open to him that would lead to freedom, if only he could outpace the terrible hunters who came on behind.

It seemed that he would never rid himself of their savage whoopings, but bit by bit, his superior stature and strength began to tell. The gauchos grew more furious in their spurrings as they realized that the stallion was outpacing them. Several began whirling their bolas to throw after him, in a vain attempt to check his flight. But the distance was too great, and the bolas swung helplessly, winding themselves about the grass tussocks and missing the white stallion's fetlocks.

Then the gauchos remembered that they had work to do on the plain behind them. Regretfully, they checked their mounts and turned them back to the scene of the hunt. The dying horses must be finished off, and all had to be skinned. They jogged back to their work, cursing the stallion that had escaped them, at the same time admiring his beauty, his speed, his grace, his wildness—everything about him. Each man, in his heart, was determined to have the albino for himself, saying nothing to his fellows.

III

When the gauchos had gone from that part of the pampa, the albino returned. More than a week had passed by, but still the fear had not left him. There was hardly any place where he could sojourn without seeing or hearing them. They were hunting over the whole district for the hides of horses or wild cattle and the feathers of the rheas. For the whole week, the albino had kept on running—first to the west, then to the north, eastward, southward—wherever he could to escape the gauchos.

Had he forgotten the terrible extermination of his herd, he would have soon been reminded by the smell of rotting carcasses that clung to the air and the sight of the heavy-bellied hawks that could not even move in their fullness.

Terror and disgust were mingled as he wheeled about the place. Once again he fled, hardly knowing where he could go to escape the slaughterers that had suddenly descended upon the tranquil pampa.

His wild eyes wide with panic, his sleek coat dank with sweat, his jaws half-open, the better to suffer his thirst-swollen tongue, he galloped from place to place, driven by fear and afraid to linger for more than a moment in any one spot. Without the hundred mares that had been his, whose carcasses were but meat for the scavengers, even loneliness terrified him.

The Lonely Beach

Once the gauchos had seen the albino stallion and found him so beautiful he knew no peace. There were men who had wanted to forsake the hunt that very day in order to chase after him, and would have done so, but that the one in charge forbade them.

"There's time enough for chasing after fancies when the work is finished," he told them. "When this is done and you've all been paid, then you can chase after a dozen white stallions if you wish."

There were arguments among them, too, about to whom the stallion belonged, for most of them coveted him.

"He's mine. I saw him first," said one.

"But if I catch him first, I shall keep him," another replied. And they squabbled and might even have ended the argument with their knives had not the one who led them been forceful in character and respected by all.

As it was, they held themselves in check until their ox wagons were creaking under the weight of skins and feathers that must be taken to town. They waited until the money had been shared between them, and they passed a few weeks spending it here and there. Then those who were still interested returned to where they had first seen the stallion, and set out in search of him.

By this time, their imaginations had increased the stallion's propensities a hundredfold. He was bigger than any animal they had ever seen, and far more beautiful; swifter than the rushing winter winds, and wilder. They repeated the story so many times that eventually they came to believe it. They convinced themselves and their listeners that the stallion was a horse like no other.

Thus, as spring mellowed into summer, any number of gauchos set out in search of him. Some rode in twos or threes, some rode singly. Some tired of searching for him and were diverted to other things. Others were steadfast, and spent the whole summer crossing and recrossing the district where first they had seen him. Eventually, he was discovered.

There was no mistaking him for another. His pure coloring, his stance, the magnificence of his features were enough to tell any gaucho—even those who had come in search of him only on hearsay—that this was the stallion they sought. But they soon discovered that it would not be easy to catch him.

The albino stallion had become the wariest of creatures now, shunning all company and made fearful by the first hoofbeat that reached his hearing. When the sound of a galloping horse came to his ears, long before it was within his sight he would be away, his ears flattened, his tail held high and streaming out behind him. Rarely did the gauchos see more than this, a fast-fleeing, cloudlike creature, far beyond their reach.

They chased him into the darkness of the nights, and in the mornings they set out in pursuit of him again. With a man behind him, the stallion never faltered. While the gauchos slept, he would still keep running.

In the darkest hours before dawn broke, he would pause a while to draw in deep breaths of air and snatch at the thistles. Then he would be away again, fear stronger than weariness or hunger.

Although the gauchos' horses were fresher than the albino, the men lost time searching for his tracks. It might take them half a day to find him. In fast pursuit, the stallion had the advantage too. He was swifter than the average pony, his legs were much longer, and he carried no weight upon his back.

The summer days lost their freshness and became sullenly hot. Dark clouds gathered at times, but a breeze would come up and push them away. The grass withered, and the ground grew hard. The stallion was weary now, and his pursuers were losing interest. Their first enthusiasm had died long since. Only determination kept them to the chase. But with the burning sun reflecting its heat from the sky and the ground, even determination wavered, and it was difficult to find the albino's tracks on the hard-baked earth.

There came a day when the stallion instinctively knew that no one was following him. He was still cautious; he still kept moving. The whole day passed without sighting a single gaucho. That night he rested and tore at the faded grass with unsatisfied hunger. The next day he was off again. He was more and more certain that no one pursued him. For two or three days, he kept up his flight. It was halfhearted now, and he stopped occasionally to graze. Only when he was finally satisfied that his enemy had left him in peace did he relax.

He grazed and dozed and grazed some more, but always his ears were alert for the slightest unusual sound.

A startled bird was all he needed to set him off at a gallop. The days passed by, and nothing happened to disturb his tranquillity. He was thin and jaded, his proud head drooped, but the victory was his. His spirit was as wild as ever.

II

Because the gauchos had been unable to capture the stallion, they could not forget him. All through the hot summer, when they spent their spare hours exchanging news at the nearest store, or lazed in the shadow of a solitary ombu tree, sipping at the maté pot with friends and circulating stories, the elusive albino was mentioned. He became renowned for his speed and beauty.

Their imagination ever dwelling in the infinite world of spirits and goblins, it did not take the gauchos long to decide that the animal was possessed. In fact, he did not exist at all, but was a demon, appearing only to torment them and lead them to their doom should they insist upon following him. To what strange world would he take them, assuming that he was never lost from sight? Could any gaucho possibly ride him, and what would become of the bold one who tried?

Such were the idle suppositions of the gauchos, haunted by their own loneliness, and populating it with unearthly beings. But even as they wondered thus, it occurred to them that he might just be a horse of flesh and blood, wilier, fleeter, more "gaucho" than their own. They spoke of taking up the chase again, when the cooler weather returned.

So it was that as the summer birds began to grow

restless, remembering the warmer northern lands, and the rivers and lakes were no longer graced with glowing flamingo colors, the gauchos were once again foraging the pampa for the albino stallion. Winter had come before they found him. He had wandered a long way southward, almost afraid of the green lands from which sprang so cruel and persistent an enemy. He had gone on and on, until the winds that tickled his nostrils brought only the scent of ice and barrenness. Then he halted. The cold was piercing, and he was not prepared for it.

He found himself among rocks and hard soil and stunted trees, where grass was difficult to discover and unsucculent. At least he found peace there, which was all he sought. His hair grew thicker as the weather worsened. He accustomed himself to the land; to winds that howled and were ever constant; to the nighttime silence—here, the ground was too hard for the vizcachas to burrow. Although he sometimes would lift his head to breathe in the winds that crossed the pampa, bringing with them a reminder of sweet alfalfa and other herbs, he stayed in this new place. There were no men there to molest him.

The days were often gray. As winter deepened, an insidious mist crept over everything, giving strange, unearthly forms to the rocks and bushes. At first, the stallion was disturbed by this strange element that clung so damply to him, and through which he could hardly see at times. The mist had a salty taste. It came in from the great Atlantic, which was not very far away, and it left a tangy flavor on the grass and bushes. There were days when the darkness hardly lifted from the land. Other days, it rained almost constantly. Although the stallion was unused to so harsh a climate, he endured it because of the sanctuary it offered him.

But even there he discovered that his tranquillity was not to last. One day, he heard the shouts of men and the wild galloping of horses' hooves. Now he was truly desperate in his fear, for it seemed that never would he be able to escape them. His lonely sojourn had not caused him to forget their callous ways and their brutality. Again he fled, not knowing where he could go in order to be rid of them forever.

The chase this time was a sporadic one. The gloomy climate protected the stallion in its way, gathering him up in the mist, which was as white as he, and hiding him even from the gauchos' piercing eyes. Seeing him disappear with such rapidity, they were even more convinced that the horse they sought to capture was but a spirit. They, also, were unaccustomed to the sea mists that descended and lifted so rapidly.

"This is a terrain fit for devils," said one, when they had pulled up their mounts in confusion, hardly able to see more than a pace or two on either side. "No wonder that we should find him here."

"Devil or not," replied another, "my three Marias will take care of him."

The "Three Marias" referred to the three stone balls of the bolas. But before they could trip up the stallion they had to be within reach of him, and in the sudden fogs it was difficult to find him. At times, the albino would be hardly more than a mile ahead, stumbling over boulders, almost unable to run. Then, when they thought he was theirs, a blanket of white mist crossed their paths and the stallion disappeared into it.

"It's a devil sent to torment us," insisted the first gaucho again. "I've never chased after any animal so long and still not been able to catch him. He'll lead us to damnation if we insist on following."

And he was all for turning back to a more Christian land, where at least a man could see where he was going. The others had more courage than their companion, and were not afraid of challenging the devil once in a while.

"Let's catch him and give him a good thrashing for our pains," they said. "We'll teach him not to be a devil."

But the days passed. Sometimes they saw him, and sometimes they only heard him. He was never far beyond their reach. Not even the stallion could travel very quickly. He rarely broke from a canter or a hurried trot. The land was rocky and loose with scree, and the mist that hid him from his pursuers also prevented him from making much progress. It seemed to the gauchos that he tormented them on purpose, always within their reach but so elusive. They cursed him and prayed to all the saints for assistance in the capture of him.

The face of the land changed again. Rocky ground gave way to sand. The few bushes and trees were all bent in a westerly direction, deformed by the constant wind. The hills were hills of sand, dunes that constantly altered in height or thickness or position, according to the wind. Desperate was the horse that trod this forsaken countryside, where not even a blade of grass would grow or a bird linger. Brave were the men who followed him, who had never seen such country-side in all their lives, and were convinced that they were pursuing the very devil to his inferno.

Now the wind blew with vengeance, whipping the breath from the stallion's open jaws, almost choking him with its force. His red eyes stung with the salt that clung to the air, his tongue was swollen with thirst. There was a crashing sound in his ears, slow, persistent, eternal—a sound he had never heard before. On he raced, not caring where he went. The gauchos were behind him, and he knew that his energy was failing fast.

That day, a strong wind blew in from the ocean. The mist lifted. The noise that had bewildered the stallion revealed itself as the motion of the sea, huge, gray waves that crashed upon the sand. Now the horse saw that he could go no farther. Ahead of him was the sea, cold, relentless. Behind him were the men.

He halted for a moment, his proud head lifted. The wind caught at the thick forelock and mane, blowing them back from his head and neck. His jaws were wide open, as were his nostrils, as he vainly tried to drag fresh energy into his burning lungs. His eyes seemed to glow in desperation.

It was thus that the gauchos suddenly saw him. They pulled up their horses, hardly able to believe what they saw. Surely there was no horse anywhere as beautiful as this one, who looked almost ready to spring up into the clouds in his effort to escape. Could this be an animal of flesh and blood, so white against the leaden sea, his eyes burning like two fires, his locks like the wings of the angels?

For several moments they hesitated, almost afraid

to pursue him further. Even as they wondered and admired and doubted, the stallion saw them and knew that he was lost. He gave a wild and desperate neigh, which rang above the sound of the crashing waves; he paced along the beach with tossing head, beautiful in his terror.

The gauchos forgot their wonder. They split into two groups, hurriedly making plans. One group galloped to the north, another to the south. On that long and lonely beach the stallion was trapped between them. They came rushing toward him from both directions, the sound of their horses' hooves thundering over the hard sand, which was flung up on every side of them.

The stallion lingered, prancing in small circles, tossing his beautiful head as if in defiance of them. Now he heard the sound of their bolas, cutting viciously through the air. It was a sound that frightened him. He knew what it represented. Within moments his freedom would be lost. They would be upon him.

He made a short run in the direction from which he had come, then changed his course, knowing that it was futile. Back he swirled again. As the gauchos drew near enough to let fly at him with their weapons, the stallion flung himself into the sea, preferring to lose himself among the heavy waters than to surrender to man.

The gauchos saw his whiteness dig deeply into the waves, which were almost black in color, reflecting the gloomy sky. For a second, his mane and tail were banners, flying freely in the wind. Then the water took them, swirling them about his body. The gauchos cried out involuntarily. The horse would be drowned!

They dragged their mounts to a halt at the edge of the sea and watched in silence as the stallion forged his way through the racing waves. Ahead of him was nothing but a wall of mist; behind him an ever-increasing distance between himself and the shore. The gauchos watched until he disappeared, lost in the sea or the mist, or both. They did not know.

"Well, that's the end of him," remarked one at last, regret in his voice.

The others were silent. Only when they were sure that the horse would not come up out of the waves again, that the adventure was surely ended, as their companion had stated, did they turn their mounts away and return inland.

The beach was lonely again, as ever it had been. When the men and horses had gone, the waves came up over the sand and washed all the hoofprints away.

Part II

The Boy

Aurelio

Several small towns had come into existence along the banks of a wide, slow river that meandered through the pampa. They populated the empty grasslands in tiny dots and were separated from each other by days of travel. The river was the same mud-brown color as the few dirt roads that crossed the towns. It was not until late afternoon, when the dying sun's rays glimmered in its waters, that the river turned to silver and gold.

It was then that Aurelio liked to slip off his clothes and slide into the river. As its chill waters crept over him, lapping gently under his chin, he imagined that he was bathing in a magic river; that the water was the sun's aura; and that his thin, tanned body was also touched with gold and silver.

It lasted but a minute, this illusion of his. But it was all he needed to feel that the dirt of the day was cleansed from his body, and with it was washed away his poverty and his dread. The gold and silver filled his pores, and gave him, anew, a sense of hope, a belief in the improbable, an illusion of happiness.

He would come up out of the water when the minute was up, and the river would be mud brown again. Sitting among the rushes and dabbing off the superfluous water with his shirt, it was as though the moment had never happened. As soon as he had pulled on his oft-darned trousers and wrapped the shirt about his shoulders, the boy's newfound hopes would vanish as rapidly as the silver and gold on the water.

There had been a time, when first he discovered the magic of the river, when his illusions would last until he got back home again, often until the following day or longer. The circumstances of his life at present weighed so heavily upon him that they could not be dispelled for more than an instant. It was difficult to have faith in magic.

It was not the everyday poverty he cared about. He had known nothing else and did not even dream of becoming rich, having no inborn desire to be so. From early childhood, he had often entertained himself by staring through the iron grilles that protected the pations of the few rich men in the town. Staring through those bars, which separated the garden from the street, was like staring in upon another world.

He saw virulent green plants, huge, shining, enticing in their freshness, which the servants dusted and polished much to Aurelio's disbelieving amusement. The roses with blooms of every color made him giddy with their perfume. The sparkling fountains with their never-ending source of water, the singing birds that decorated the shadows, and the mosaic tiles, which were far too beautiful to be trodden on—all this Aurelio appreciated and admired without wanting any of it for himself. He was happy to know that such a world existed and that he could partake of it, if only from outside, in the dusty, unpaved street. He felt it was as much his as the rich man's. The bars disappeared as he stared, because he had no resentment of them.

Sometimes, he watched the rich men come out of

their small palaces, and step into their polished carriages or mount glossy, pure-blooded horses. The men were immaculately clothed themselves, and their mounts equalled them in grooming and expensive bits and saddles. Often the rich men, seeing him, would search in their pockets and throw the boy a coin. He would recover it with dignity, not groveling like the other lads who sometimes gathered around also.

He was poor, he had nothing material to call his own. But he was not a beggar and had no need of money. Aurelio had always been content with the shack in which he lived, the straw-packed mattress that was his bed, and the aunt he adored as the only person who belonged to him and loved him.

It was only now, when he was fifteen, that Aurelio began to feel the weight of his poverty. Now, because his aunt was ill, and between them they could afford not even the worst doctor in the town to attend her. Now, because he knew—although she insistently denied it—that she would die and he would be left alone.

Oh, it was delicious to sink into the river up to his chin, and for a moment be a child again, lapped by its sun-touched magic! But the minute he was on the bank, shivering slightly in the sudden chill of the early evening, he was no longer a child easily deluded by dreams, but a boy with the problems of a man upon his shoulders.

II

Aurelio knew that his future was as murky as the river. From whence the river came and where it was going, he had no knowledge. And hardly more did he know about himself. The only realities in his life, apart from his joy in living and his ability to appreciate both simple and beautiful things, were his aunt and the adobe hut that had always been his home.

There was a wooden chest containing a few clothes. Most of them had belonged to his mother and were now worn by his aunt. One dress remained untouched. It was made of dark green velvet, magically soft to the touch, although the years were robbing it of both its softness and its luster. Aurelio's mother had worn it on her wedding day. She wore it also when she ran away from home. It was the kind of dress that wives and daughters of rich men wore. Aurelio's mother had suffered poverty for only a very short time.

Besides the chest, there was nothing but a bed, a table, and two chairs. The chest stood beneath the only window the hut possessed. On it was a plaster statue of a saint in whom his aunt had faith. The candle beside it was the only illumination they had at night. There was not even a fireplace, and the cooking had to be done in an oven outside.

Aurelio's aunt was his mother's sister. He called her Tia Luisa. All that he knew about her was that she was older than his mother and that she had been as devoted to her as she now was to him.

Thinking about his aunt, Aurelio hardly noticed that the river had grown darker in the falling shadows of the night. She would be in the house now, waiting for him. She would be lying on the bed, trying to pretend, even to herself, that her constant weakness was due to the heat of the long summer days. His breast swelled with pain; he loved her so dearly. In spite of his dip in the river, he still had not the courage to return and see the incurable weariness in her face.

Dear Tia Luisa! He had no one else. His mother was dead. His father—who knew what had become of him? He had fled from the house, half crazed with grief and remorse, never to return. Tia Luisa had once told him that his father was a wild man. "All gauchos are. They're as uncomfortable living like ordinary people in towns and houses as the savage mustangs they ride would be."

"An ill-fated pair were your parents," she often said, sighing and blinking the tears from her eyes. She had loved them equally, and threw no blame on Aurelio's father, even though he had never returned to see his son.

Then she would explain for the thousandth time how she and her sister had gone to visit the *estancia* of a friend of their father; how her sister had fallen madly in love with an impressionable young gaucho who happened to be working there at the time. They ran away to be married in some country church, miles from anywhere, so that her father could not find them and stop the wedding. Eventually, they came to this town because Aurelio was to be born. His mother wanted to make a home for him. Aurelio never tired of the story, which was as romantic as anything his imagination could desire.

As soon as her sister had sent for her, Tia Luisa came in spite of their raging father. She stayed on, after her sister died, to look after the baby. She sold all of her finery, bit by bit, to keep herself and the child alive. Pride restrained her from writing to her family for assistance. Anyway, her father would neither forgive nor understand. He would be capable of leaving the baby in an orphanage, unwanted.

In the first years, there were several offers of marriage. She was young and attractive, and obviously well bred. When she refused to give up the baby, her suitors became disinterested. Tia Luisa remained alone.

She began to do fine embroidery and lacework for the gentle ladies of the town. But it was a complicated, endless task that earned her very little money. She took in coarser sewing as Aurelio grew and needed more food. The ladies, taking pity on her, offered to let her wash their linen, if she promised to be careful with it.

Now that she was ill, Aurelio could understand the many sacrifices she had made for him. He cared so much that it hurt, and it hurt because he knew he could do nothing for her in return. He recalled how she was always busy and often tired. On washing days, the neat bun would fall apart, the strands of her black hair, streaked with gray, drooping over her face and sticking to her cheeks and forehead. When she was sewing, she looked serene and lovely, like a grand lady in her parlor. But she had long ago sacrificed her right to such a title.

She even found time to educate Aurelio a little. She taught him to read and write. The only book they possessed was the Bible, and Aurelio had read it almost from end to end, fascinated by the stories, events, and characters unfolded on nearly every one of its fine rice-paper pages. She told him stories that she herself had read; she opened his mind to a world that existed beyond the boundaries of this small pampa town. His rich imagination was succored by what he read and heard.

He thought he had wasted his days. Instead of dreaming and playing, he should have been caring for Tia Luisa, finding some way of relieving her of her tasks. So often he had made fine promises of how he would look after her when he grew to manhood. He was almost a man, and still he had done nothing, nor knew what he could do.

Aurelio watched the river, hunching his shoulders as if to better bear the weight that dragged him down. The river moved so slowly, so patiently; it had always done so and would long after he was gone. There seemed to be some kind of message in the river, if only he could understand it. He would follow it one day, find out where it went. Perhaps where the river ended, he would find his destiny.

There was a road that ran alongside the river for many miles, a cart-track, deeply rutted by the wheels of the big ox-drawn carts that passed by from time to time. It was the road that all travelers first took on leaving the town. His own father had taken this track to go . . . where?

Perhaps the road would take him to his father. Imagination at last won over his problems. He began to smile as dusk settled over the river, and the rushes on its banks became thin silhouettes. He would find his father and bring him to Tia Luisa, and together they would start a new life. Somehow, Tia Luisa would be a lady again.

In Pursuit of a Dream

Had Tia Luisa been well, Aurelio might have set out the very next day on what had suddenly become, in his imagination, a great adventure. He went home that evening, his head racing with visions. It seemed, after all, that the magic of the river had not failed him. He felt himself capable of doing anything and everything.

When he reached the hut, one of a straggling line on the edge of the checkerboard town, his aunt was not outside tending the oven or sewing, and no glimmer of a candle lighted the doorway. The boy's heart sank at this reminder of his aunt's illness. Almost with dread, he approached his home, and softly entered.

"Is that you, Aurelio?" His aunt's voice came from the dark corner and sounded faint.

"Yes, Tia Luisa."

"Light the candle. It's so dark in here. I must have been asleep and didn't notice how the sun has gone down."

Aurelio fumblingly obeyed. He was clumsy in his dread. These days he was almost afraid to see his aunt's face in the candlelight, so wan and hollow had it become.

The meager flame sprang up and sank into a steady glow and shadows moved jerkily on the four rough walls of the hut. Aurelio went over to the bed and sat down beside his aunt, taking one of her hands in his own.

"Where have you been, my son?"

"By the river."

"You're always by the river. What do you do there?"

"I think."

"And what do you think?"

"About you. About. . . ."

The ideas had suddenly gone from his head. Looking down on Tia Luisa's face, a mere shadow on the pillow, he knew he could not go away and leave her.

"Nothing," he said. "Just things."

Tia Luisa sighed. She stroked the boy's hand that clasped hers and said softly, "Thinking can be painful sometimes."

"If you were well. . . ," began Aurelio, his vision starting up again at the encouraging gentleness of her touch.

"I will get well, Aurelio. This is just a passing ailment. A short rest in bed is all I need." She paused and then added, "And what do you think of doing when I'm well?"

"I thought of going to look for my father."

"Oh, Aurelio!" Disappointment sounded in Tia Luisa's voice. "But that's only a dream. You're too old for dreams. How could you ever find him? How would you even know him?"

"If he's alive I will find him. And if I found him, I would know him."

Aurelio spoke almost violently. Perhaps it was a dream, but it was the only one that made his life bearable. But he did not pronounce this thought to his aunt. It would have hurt her too much.

"You must find a job, Aurelio. That's what you need to look for now."

The boy said nothing. He had tried three jobs. With his knowledge of reading and writing, he had been able to find employment as a minor clerk with three different companies, but, with all the will in the world, he had been unable to endure being pinioned to a high stool, copying figures or lists, imprisoned in a musty, paper-crowded room. After a week or so, something inside him had exploded and he'd had to leave.

He had to be out in the air, surrounded by space, not walls. For all the education his aunt had given him, his own restless nature made it worthless to him.

But he said determinedly, "I will, Tia Luisa. There must be something I can do."

They smiled at each other in the half-darkness, but neither was deceived. Tia Luisa knew that Aurelio would not find a job, and Aurelio knew that Tia Luisa would not get better.

The woman gently disentangled her hand from the boy's grasp. She waved toward the door.

"Go and heat up the stew," she said. "You must be hungry. We might as well eat."

Aurelio went outside. The fireplace was filled with ashes that were still warm. He added a small amount of fuel, blew up a flame with the help of the candle, and put the earthenware pot over the heat. The stew contained chunks of tough cow meat, a couple of potatoes, and rice grains that had sunk to the bottom. The rest were spices, which helped to disguise the taste.

While he waited for the pot to warm and for steam to rise up from the water, he returned to thinking of the idea that had come to him by the river. Tia Luisa's words came back to him too. "You're too old for dreams. How could you ever find him?" Was it only a dream?

II

Tia Luisa survived the wearying heat of the summer. There were days when she felt quite strong and even got through all the sewing that had been left to her as well as some of the washing. People did not leave much washing for her now. She tired rapidly, bent over the big earthenware tub, and often had to leave the things unwashed. Then the people would complain because the clothes were not ready when they wanted them, and next time they sent them somewhere else.

Aurelio earned a few coins writing letters for people who were too ignorant to write their own. But there were not many people among his acquaintances who needed to write at all. He ran errands and risked his hard-earned centavos gambling on the street corners with the other lads, hoping to augment his income, and sometimes succeeding. But always he was haunted by hunger and his aunt's growing weakness.

Tia Luisa also survived the autumn rains and the long damp months of winter. She hardly moved from her bed on many of those days, and she spoke in a whisper. Half the night would be spent coughing. Aurelio would wrap their one blanket tightly about her, protecting her in fear and agonized love. Their only hope was for the coming of spring, when the weather would grow more clement. Surely Tia Luisa's cough would abate then, and she would regather her strength in the sunshine.

Spring came. But it came too late to save Tia Luisa. No amount of sun could bring balm to her tortured lungs. She had not the energy to rise from the bed and drag herself to the door to see the fresh blueness of the sky. Even if she could have done so, the powerful air would have overwhelmed her. Aurelio hung around the house, afraid to leave her. Sometimes the neighbors would come with homemade medicines. Tia Luisa would swallow them with difficulty but with gratitude. The same neighbors would offer the boy a plateful of whatever poor meal they had made for themselves.

Sometimes he would go down to the river, but now he never saw it change to gold and silver. The water was muddy, cold, and gloomy. He would stare at the cart-track and knew that soon, very soon, he would be free to follow it.

Tia Luisa died so quietly one night that Aurelio was unaware of it until the following morning. The grief in his heart was too hard to allow tears to fall. He knelt beside the bed and held her frozen hand in his own for a long time. Thus he was discovered by the neighbor who had come with her usual medicine and inquiry. She disentangled the boy from his aunt's side and sent him on various errands to keep him from thinking. By the time the coldness had melted from his heart, and he could feel again, Tia Luisa had been buried pauper fashion, and Aurelio was completely alone.

He wandered about the streets, afraid to return to the house. When he stopped to gaze through the railings into the rich men's gardens, he saw no flowers or singing birds or beautiful tiles. All was a blur to him. His dark eyes were blinded by tears.

Eventually he found himself by the river. On its bank he passed empty, despairing hours, pulling savagely at the rushes. He was unaware of time or the existence of anything outside himself and the sorrow which overwhelmed him, until the creaking sound of wheels brought his attention to the swaying, overloaded ox-cart that passed him on the opposite bank. The black-and-white beasts were slow-moving, heedless of the driver who prodded them with a cane.

A couple of gauchos rode alongside the cart, which was loaded to overspilling with hides of many colors. Aurelio stared at the gauchos. With their hats pulled low over their bearded faces and hunched in ponchos that came down to their knees, they seemed a part of the drooping-headed horses they rode. The last of the day's sunshine glinted for a moment on the big spurs that were tied to the naked heels of one and the rough, toeless boots of the other.

Something stirred in Aurelio's heart, something deeper and stronger than the sorrow that flooded him. One of these men could be his father. From their kind he himself had sprung, and to them he belonged. Tia Luisa had taught him to read and write. The town itself had tried to form his character to its ways. But always he had been an outsider, incapable of sitting at an office desk, drawn always to the river and the open pampa beyond, which had been calling him so subtly that until this moment he had not recognized its call.

The wish to find his father—was that, too, just part of the call? Was it his gaucho blood that made him uneasy in the town? Aurelio's heaviness suddenly left him. There was a yearning that overcame his heartache. Now his destiny was clear.

III

"Yes," agreed the hostler at the stable in the town. "I can sell you a horse easily enough."

He started at Aurelio, noticing the patches and tears in his clothes, the hungry thinness of his face.

"I can even give you a horse if you like."

He laughed at the eager light that came to the boy's eyes.

"It's not the horse that costs money, lad. You buy the saddle and bridle, and I'll throw in a horse free of charge." As an afterthought he added, "I suppose you can ride?"

"Of course," retorted Aurelio with all the dignity he could master. It would never do for a prospective gaucho to admit that he had never been on the back of a horse in all his life. "How much do you want for the saddle and bridle?"

The man told him, and Aurelio promised to return just as soon as he had raised the money. He went back to the hut in which he had been born, mustered together all the possessions contained within, including the green velvet dress that had belonged to his mother, put them outside, and offered them to any interested passerby.

The amount he eventually collected was pitifully small. There was no one in that district with money to spare for any unnecessary article. Aurelio returned to the horse-dealer with less than the money he needed.

For a long time the hostler hesitated. Aurelio, in his innocence, dreaded that he would be turned away. But eventually the man said, "Well, bearing in mind you're only a lad, and having a fondness for young people and a generous heart, I'll make a deal with you. You can have the saddle and bridle and also the horse. Of course, he can't be as good a horse as I would have offered you. You understand that, I suppose?"

"Oh, yes!" cried Aurelio, ready to agree to anything in his eagerness to set out on his great adventure.

The man motioned to the boy to follow him. In the dark corner of a foul-smelling stall, Aurelio dimly made out the shadow of a horse.

"That's him. And a bargain for the money you've got. He might not be a beauty and he might not be so young, but he's a horse and that's what you're needing."

The hostler led out the horse, plunking down a dirty, shabby-looking woolen saddle over its back as he did so. In the daylight Aurelio saw that it was astonishingly gaunt and bald in patches. He was too ignorant of horses to notice the rheumy eyes, the sagging quarters, and the general ill-appearance of the animal. It was not the splendid animal he had imagined himself possessing, but it was better than nothing and all he could afford for the time being.

"Has it got a name?" he said to the man, unable to think of any complimentary remark or to even feel it necessary to thank him.

"Mouse," said the man, "and a good beast he is for all that he doesn't look up to much."

He draped a badly mended bridle about the horse's head, pulled up the saddle girth, and handed the reins into Aurelio's hands. Meanwhile, Mouse seemed indifferent to all that occurred.

Aurelio handed over the money and, anxious that the hostler should not be aware of his ignorance of horses, preferred to lead the animal down the street and out of sight of the stable before attempting to mount him.

"We make a fine pair, Mouse and I," thought Aurelio with a grimace, as the horse almost staggered beneath his weight. But his heart was light as the horse plodded along the street, bearing him toward the river and the cart-track that wound its way across the pampa. Even though Mouse swayed and seemed to have the gait of a cow, even though Aurelio felt uncomfortable in the saddle and hardly knew how to manage the reins that were harsh and too big for his fingers, he was borne up by a sense of anticipation, and excitement burned within him.

He felt no regrets about leaving the town. He had no special friends to say goodbye to or to miss. Ahead of him was freedom, the life of a gaucho that he was determined to make his own. Perhaps—if fate were kind to him—he would also fulfill the dream that Tia Luisa had gently derided.

Santa Clara

Don Jacinto Negrin, owner of the Estancia Santa Clara, looked down from his horse at the boy who had asked him for a job. He saw a thin-faced, exhausted lad whose town clothes were dirty and tattered, whose shoes were broken and laceless, loosely holding the reins of a creature he assumed to be a horse and looked as broken and tattered and exhausted as its owner. In spite of the boy's youth and weariness and semistarved appearance, there was something about him that spoke in his favor. Perhaps it was no more than the bright hope that shone in the dark, hunger-shadowed eyes, and the lack of humility, in spite of the obvious need.

"What's your name?" said Don Jacinto as coldly as he could. He wanted no beggars or scoundrels on his land.

Aurelio told him.

"And where do you come from?"

Aurelio answered politely, without forsaking his dignity despite his shabbiness and the scornful look that the *estanciero* directed at him.

"Why do you come here looking for work? Have you run away from home? There's no place here for thieves or vagabonds."

"I'm neither one nor the other," retorted Aurelio, stung by the man's injustice, and he turned his back on Don Jacinto, preparing to mount again and look in another place for a job.

"Wait," demanded Don Jacinto. "Don't run off so fast. This is the only place near here where the dogs are fat; you'll fare far worse somewhere else. Tell me what you can do and I'll tell you if there's work for you."

"Anything," said Aurelio. "And what I don't know I'll soon learn."

The man liked the spirited sound of his reply. For the first time he laughed and looked in a kindlier fashion at the boy.

"Very well, then. Go to the kitchen and get yourself something to eat. You'll find the majordomo there. His name's Serafin. Ask for him and say I've just employed you. And make sure you work. The dogs may be fat but they earn their keep."

"And so shall I."

"Colt!" cried the man. "Wait till you've felt the whip and spurs," but he laughed to himself as he watched the boy walk slowly toward the house, his gait obviously that of one who has ridden too far and is unaccustomed to the saddle.

II

There was nothing grand about the Estancia Santa Clara. Don Jacinto was a bachelor, and the adobe hut that had originally been the estancia house was still enough for him. Its three dark rooms were roofed with thatch; its floors were hard earth over which hens wandered and pecked, fleas and bugs jumped, and dogs sprawled gnawing at bones. There was a rough bed, piled with dirty sheepskins, on which the owner presumably slept. The middle room contained a few shabby chairs, a wooden chest, and some faded prints tacked to the walls, including two pictures of the gaucho president, Rosas. The third room was the kitchen.

The kitchen was the friendliest room in the house, though no cleaner than the rest. A fireplace fed its flames into a huge chimney and was big enough to roast a lamb or a calf on the spit. There was a long pine table with benches on either side, a few greasy sheepskins scattered about the corners where a gaucho occasionally slept when the weather was inclement, and the smoke-grimed walls offered uncertain refuge to insects of every kind.

This was to be Aurelio's home. The fifteen gauchos who worked for Don Jacinto gathered here in the early hours of the morning, before the sun could touch upon the pampa and dispel the mists of spring and summer, to pass around the maté pot and discuss the work of the coming day.

Some would stay behind to mend a broken bridle or saddle girth. Most of them would be off within minutes of the given order, spurring their half-wild ponies and yelling like Indians to make them buck and rear with flattened ears. Aurelio soon discovered that there was nothing a gaucho liked more than to start the day battling with his horse.

The other gauchos would watch and join in the yelling, sometimes flailing the bucking animal with their own whips to make it fight more. Aurelio would watch with admiration the skill of the rider, so much a part of his mount that nothing the horse could do would dislodge him. If only he could ride like that! Then, and then only, would he have the right to call himself "gaucho" as they did.

He felt like an outsider when he watched these early morning displays. Not only was he a very incompetent rider, but he did not even have a horse capable of springing two inches from the ground. Poor old Mouse almost collapsed every time the boy mounted him, and one screech from a nearby gaucho was enough to set him trembling.

The other men laughed at Aurelio's mount and called the poor brute names. Aurelio was ashamed of the horse and longed for a better one, but he was fond of him and would not have him suffer any ill. This sentiment he kept to himself, of course. The gauchos ridiculed him enough as it was, in spite of the rough affection with which they had immediately accepted him.

He felt like an outsider, too, because of the clothes he wore, town clothes, even though they were tattered and fit only for a beggar. He wanted to dress like the gauchos, with a pair of long, white cotton pants trimmed with a deep border of lace, and a length of colored cloth to wind around his waist and between his legs, over the pants, with a belt to keep it from slipping. He wanted a poncho in place of his jacket with its frayed elbows. There would be neither pants, *chiripá* nor poncho, until he had earned himself some money to pay for them. The majordomo, Serafin, had suggested that he buy these things at the nearest store, in a small village some ten miles away. He had too much respect for the boy's pride to offer him the loan of a few pesos.

Instead, he told him to watch the men when they brought in a cow for killing, so that he might learn to kill and to skin such an animal; to watch the *domador* —the horse breaker—with the wild mustangs, to learn his tricks if not his skill. He gave the boy harness to mend, told him to keep up the stock of fuel for the fire, and found many a trifle to keep him busy around the house. Aurelio complied with all that was asked of him, though often he was impatient and sullen because he had not ridden so far to watch other men work and wait on them.

But one day, after he had been at the estancia for about a fortnight, the majordomo said to him, "There's a bay horse in the corral. Don Jacinto says that it's yours if you can ride it, in payment for the work you've done."

Aurelio's heart leaped with excitement at these words. He could hardly contain himself from running out to the corral to see the horse. It was becoming an embarrassment to ride Mouse, and almost a cruelty. The poor beast grew weaker in spite of the good grass he was eating and the little effort he was called upon to make.

"Wait!" commanded the old gaucho, smiling at the boy's eagerness. "I'll come with you."

The corral was only a few yards away from the house. But it did not become a gaucho to walk, and so the majordomo and the boy mounted their respective horses and rode over to it. There was only the bay horse there, so Aurelio could make no mistake. At first, he was disappointed because the animal was as ugly as Mouse, though in much better condition and obviously much younger.

"There he is!" said the gaucho. "He's only been ridden a few times and, so far, has no respect for whip or spur. In spite of his looks, he's a tough beast and intelligent. He'll make a good mount if you learn how to handle him."

These were a lot of words from a man who always pondered deeply before opening his mouth. Aurelio's heart sank as he heard them. This was obviously a joke of the patron's. He looked at the roman-nosed, small-eared bay, who had stopped his eternal pacing about the corral to return the boy's stare with bright but wary eyes.

"Well," said the gaucho. "Don't you want him? Have you so many horses that you need no more, even as a gift?"

Aurelio looked at the majordomo, stirred by his sarcasm. But there was a twinkle in the old man's eyes as he said, "There's no one to see you. I'll help you this first time if you wish."

The boy nodded. He licked his lips, which had suddenly gone dry. He followed the gaucho into the corral, watching with envy the ease with which he caught the horse with his lasso and pulled him up to the snubbing post in the center of the corral.

"Get a saddle on him quickly and cinch him up tight," snapped the gaucho, keeping the rope taut.

Aurelio hurried to obey. Aware of Serafin's critical eyes, he had no time to think of fear or awkwardness.

He got the saddle on the wild-eyed bay, noticing how the horse trembled and held himself tight against what he knew would come next.

"And a halter," called the majordomo.

There was one hanging over the fence. Aurelio approached the horse's head and got the halter around his ears and muzzle.

"Now! Up on his back, and hold on with your knees and your hands for all you're worth."

Aurelio dared not disobey. His heart was in his stomach, and it churned enough to make him dizzy. But he was on the horse's back. The majordomo slackened the rope that held the bay still. Within half a second, Aurelio saw sky and earth and corral bars, and the blurred outline of the gaucho on his horse. The hard ground seemed to split his every bone, and to rock violently for an interminable period.

The gaucho was saying something, but Aurelio could not make out his words. After a while, he was aware of the bay horse standing beside him, looking down at him with what appeared to be an expression of amusement. Now he heard the gaucho shouting, "Up again. Don't waste time. I've got work to do."

Aurelio dragged himself upright, and somehow got back into the saddle. Hardly had he tangled his fingers in the horse's mane when, once again, he was on the ground, stunned and sick and aching.

"Keep at it, boy," he heard the gaucho say, penetrating the mists that clouded his pounding head. He blinked the tears from his eyes, ashamed that the old man should see them.

III

Aurelio obeyed the majordomo. Every morning he rose reluctantly from his sheepskin bed. After partaking of the hot and bitter maté, which was all the gauchos ate for breakfast, he took saddle and halter and went to the corral to begin his daily battle with the bay horse. Serafin no longer watched or helped. Aurelio knew loneliness and pain, anger and frustration.

Every day the gelding defeated him. The boy's body was covered with bruises, and he could hardly walk. His hands were swollen and stiff with the cuts that the horse's wiry mane had sliced into them. But at least the gauchos forbore from asking him how he progressed. Neither did they make fun of him, as was their wont.

Sometimes Aurelio would watch the domador with a horse brought newly from the pampa. He marvelled to see how this man could stay astride, in spite of all that the savage, frightened animal could do. If occasionally he was unseated or the horse fell, the man never sprawled disgracefully to the ground as Aurelio did, but landed always on his feet and was on the horse's back again even before the animal itself could scramble to all fours. It looked so easy, but Aurelio, sore and aching, knew otherwise.

He despaired of ever learning to ride the horse and hated him with a bitter hatred. In the few seconds that he managed to stay on his back, he would punish him with the whip the majordomo had given him.

Sometimes at night it was hard to restrain the tears

that choked within, so weary and pain-racked was his body. Then he would think of Tia Luisa and long for her and the old days. He remembered only the pleasant times and the times that he swam in the river. The only pain he ever felt then was that of hunger. He wondered why he had wanted to be a gaucho, or how he had come to believe that the life they led was romantic and exciting.

It was hard and comfortless and pain-filled. Only the poor horse, Mouse, gave him any comfort. Perhaps the horse reminded him of that other life, when he was a town boy, longing for the pampa.

He lost all count of time and place. His world was the bay gelding and his daily battle with it. There came a time when even the pain of his cuts and bruises faded, so strong was his hatred and his determination to conquer the stubborn animal. Eventually he succeeded. He never knew how long it took him or how it happened.

One late afternoon, after he had clung for what seemed an eternity, his head thrown back and forth as if he were a broken-backed marionette, his teeth occasionally biting his tongue, he suddenly felt the fight go out of the animal. He knew he had won. A wild feeling of glory and power surged through him. He thrashed the faltering animal with his whip. For the first time he cried out like the gauchos—a shrill excited sound which he uttered unconsciously. He was the victor now.

The horse bucked a few more paces, then came to a standstill, head drooping, flanks heaving, no longer caring what the boy did. Aurelio yanked the gelding's head up with the reins, stabbed his heels into his flanks, and made the gelding circle the corral, three, four, five times around, until he was sure that the horse obeyed him and knew that he was master. Then, utterly weary, the giddy joy of triumph gone, he almost fell from the horse's back, staggered to the fence, and clung there, retching.

He told no one of his victory, but somehow they knew. Perhaps it was the proud light in his eyes, or perhaps it was because the majordomo no longer heard him groaning and suppressing weary sobs in the night. Still he had not ridden the horse in front of them, but all of them knew that he had mastered it.

One morning five or six days later, he found on the floor beside his sleeping place a pile of clothing. Wonderingly, he took hold of the separate pieces—a gray woollen poncho with black stripes, a dark blue length of cloth—the chiripá—and a pair of lace-bordered pants, stiff with newness. There was even a new white shirt, a blue neckcloth, and a wide leather belt.

The gauchos had left him alone to discover their gift. The boy was glad, for his emotions were shamefully unmanly. He threw off his town clothes, and donned the others. He even put on the poncho, although it was not cold. Only his town shoes were out of place and he kicked them off. Many of the gauchos went barefoot and so could he.

At last he gathered the courage to go outside. The gauchos, busy with their mounts, pretended not to notice his new clothes. Aurelio went to the corral where the horse was waiting for him, and began the ritual of the day: saddling, haltering, mounting.

The horse began to buck and toss as usual, but Aurelio, confident in his victory and his new clothes, punished him with the whip and encouraged his wildness. For several minutes the two fighters flung about the corral together. Soon the boy, overconfident and unsuspecting, found himself sailing through the air and landing with a crash against the corral bars.

For a minute he was completely stunned, and came to at the sound of hilarious laughter. He shook the dust from his eyes and saw that most of the gauchos had watched his performance. Their utter delight at his downfall was almost infantile and for a moment pride and anger surged hotly through him.

He painfully pulled himself to his feet, longing to think of some sarcastic remark to fling at them as he beat the dust out of his new clothes. But their laughter was infectious and soon he too was laughing.

His reaction was greatly appreciated by them. Their laughter became whoops and screeches as they spurred their horses and galloped off to work. One of them flung back a remark that completely dispelled any shame Aurelio might have felt.

"I thought it was just the clothes that were 'gaucho' but it looks as though the boy inside them might be 'gaucho,' too."

It was Serafin who spoke, and Aurelio's heart swelled with pride and happiness. He went up to the bay gelding, waiting patiently for him this time and with no great willingness to fight.

"Come on, *bicho*, I'll teach you who's the boss." As he mounted, he felt something akin to affection for the animal. The horse had, after all, given him a footing into the gauchos' world where he wished to belong.

Lessons and Legends

In the days before barbed-wire fencing was introduced to the pampa, all the creatures that dwelt there roamed wherever fancy led them. The Estancia Santa Clara had no clearly marked boundaries except on its southern side, where a river divided it from another man's land. The semiwild cattle and sheep, bearing the brand of Don Jacinto, were kept from wandering by the gauchos who herded them to new pastures and kept them from straying.

For the best part of the year, the job was almost a sinecure. There was little to do but circle slowly around the scattered herd, urge on a few laggers, and stop the bulls from killing each other. Some kept guard at night, while others slept nearby beside a fire, built to discourage marauding lions, to roast meat, and to boil the kettle for the maté.

The gauchos took with them seven or eight horses, changing three times a day and leaving the rest under the guardianship of their bell mare. The bell mare was usually of light coloring or of pinto markings, so that she could be found easily in the dark. She wore a bell around her neck to which the other horses of the troop soon became accustomed and always followed. Each mare had a bell with a different tone, which was instantly recognized by the troop. The mare was hobbled, but otherwise left to wander at will. This way the gauchos were able to leave their horses to graze as they pleased without needing to worry about losing them.

When Aurelio was first allowed to ride out with the gauchos to care for the herd, he had two horses, Mouse and the bay gelding, which he had named Bicho. At first he felt pride at possessing two horses when so recently he had none at all. He soon realized that two horses were nothing. A gaucho's pride was in the number of horses he possessed, and the fact that all should be similar in coloring. Mouse hardly counted as a horse at all and was of mealy coloring, while Bicho was a bay. Most of the gauchos possessed at least thirty horses and never traveled without seven or eight of them.

At first, however, Aurelio hardly worried about his beggarly position. He and Bicho still had a lot to learn, and it was some time before a whole day spent in the saddle stopped causing him agony. Prestige made him whip up the bay every morning to make him toss and kick in company with the other mounts, though his aching back and muscles cried out against every jerk, and occasionally he disgraced himself by being unseated.

Bicho had no more idea of cattle herding than Aurelio had. It was just as well that in the early months there was nothing to do but circle the herd and keep clear of the large, savage horns the wild cows shook whenever the shadow of horse or man fell over them. Now and again, the majordomo would lend Aurelio one of his horses, partly to give Bicho a rest—Aurelio never bothered to ride Mouse any more, and only brought him along for show—and partly because an experienced horse could teach an inexperienced rider quite a few things about handling cattle.

The summer went by, and Aurelio learned. He learned to swing the bolas, though he was rarely capable of ensnaring the animal. "Keep at it, boy," the majordomo would say. Aurelio kept at it, practicing with poor Mouse who came in handy, after all, and was endlessly patient when Aurelio tangled his legs in the whirling stone balls and leather.

He learned to pick out a cow from the herd without unduly alarming her, and drive her to the gauchos, whose knives were waiting to butcher her. He learned to give signals to Bicho by touching his neck with the rein, or by the lightest pressure of knees or heels to his flanks. And the novice was patient with Bicho, who was learning too.

Aurelio learned to build a fire, to make the maté, to skin a beast and prepare it for roasting, and to eat his meat gaucho fashion, putting a chunk between his teeth and slicing through it with his knife, without cutting off his nose. As the knife had a blade some eighteen inches long, this was no mean feat.

His new clothes were baptized with dust and sweat and grease. By the end of summer, he felt he had the right to call himself a gaucho. He did not say this aloud to anyone, still it gave him great satisfaction.

Aurelio was not always learning. There were times when he had nothing to do—at the end of the day, perhaps, both he and Bicho were released from bondage, the horse to graze and he to throw himself down by the fire to either think or not, as he chose. He would watch the flames burn down to glowing embers. At times a surge of loneliness would come over him, remembering the old oven, his home, and Tia Luisa.

It was another world, and now seemed as distant as the moon that sailed silently over the earth at night. Aurelio would watch the moon and sometimes wonder at it. The moon made him feel lonely too. It emphasized the extreme emptiness of the vast, unending pampa, treeless, almost houseless, going on to an invisible horizon. The crazy widow bird would sob at night. It sounded like the sobs of a desperately unhappy woman. The gauchos shared Aurelio's loneliness and drew closer to the fire, some glancing about warily in fear of ghosts or bad spirits that were supposed to dwell in those regions at night.

One of the gauchos would say that the crazy widow bird was a bewitched woman. "She was captured by the Indians and taken to live among them, after she had seen her husband tortured and killed. So much did she wail and weep, that the Indians tired of hearing her and, to punish her, she was turned into a bird and doomed to eternal loneliness."

The other gauchos stirred uneasily on hearing this tale, and not one of them did not believe it. Although they were Christians, they had lived too long in the wilderness and among animals to be able to shake off primitive fears and imaginings. Even Aurelio, in spite of his education, in spite of his fifteen years in the town, shivered and half believed. Who could not believe when these fierce, callous, half-savage companions of his crossed themselves and were frightened?

In the mornings, before the sun was more than a suspicion of gray light in the east and the moon held sway in the sky, the embers were stirred to life to heat up the kettle. Aurelio forgot his fears and loneliness, roused by the sharp air, warmed by the fellowship of the maté pot, as it passed from hand to hand and each imbibed through the same silver tube. Hardly anyone spoke at that hour of the day and the only sounds were those of the horses who whickered to greet the advancing dawn, or a cow lowing softly to a hungry calf. It was a good time of day, fresh, clean, and bracing, when spirits no longer wandered, and God lighted up the world with His glory.

II

Aurelio had not forgotten his original purpose, made at the riverside—it seemed an eternity ago—for coming to the pampa. He was determined to find his father, even if it meant relating his tale to every single gaucho he met. At the beginning, he was a nobody, too unproven, to expect their attention to anything he said. He was too shy to speak boldly of a subject so close to his heart. Besides, he had been busy learning, and was tired and often aching.

But by the time his new clothes were as shabby-looking as those of his companions, and he had Bicho more or less educated as well as himself, when he felt that he was an accepted member of the company and had won their affection, then Aurelio did speak of his father and ask the gauchos if they knew anything of him.

He hardly expected to be successful in his search from the beginning, and it was just as well. Although the gauchos reached back in their memories, none of them could recall a man who might have been Aurelio's father. Not even Serafin, who was older than the rest and had traveled from one end of the pampa to the other, had any such memory.

"Perhaps he went over to the Indians," suggested the old gaucho. "It's the only place a gaucho can hide."

"But why should he want to hide?" asked Aurelio.

The idea of a man living voluntarily among the Indians was beyond him. He had, as yet, seen but a few in the town, domesticated Indians who had been captured in battles. They were called servants, but in reality they were slaves and had come to the town in cages, like wild animals.

Every civilized person was afraid of the Indians. Many of the ranchos and estancias were surrounded by moats or wide ditches to keep them at bay, and had lookout towers, even cannons. The Indians were masters of diabolic tortures, and were as cruel to their own race as to the Christians. The fact that most of the gauchos had Indian blood was overlooked by them, and they were the Indians' greatest enemy, almost as savage, and as skilled in horsemanship, lance-throwing, and hand-to-hand killing as the Indians.

"If a man disappears for fifteen years," the major-domo told Aurelio, "the chances are that he went over to the Indians. Otherwise, he would have turned up again. Perhaps they murdered him; or perhaps they accepted him, and he died of one of their diseases or of their foul medicines."

A gloomy death was the most salutary end to any story, Aurelio was to learn. None of the gauchos could proffer a better solution. Aurelio asked the horse breaker, for he was a man who traveled from place to place, and brought news from the outside to the estancia. But even he could tell Aurelio nothing. For the present, the boy was no nearer to completing his mission than he had been that day by the riverside.

Meanwhile, the seasons passed. Aurelio continued to learn. There was the branding of the new calves in spring and the occasional, wearisome treks to some town, driving a herd of two or three hundred head of cattle to the stockyards and slaughterhouses.

The first trip for Aurelio was in midwinter. If he thought he had learned all there was of enduring and suffering, he discovered that he was mistaken. The trip took two weeks to complete, and it rained every day out of the fourteen. The gauchos could light no fires at any stopping place. Their clothes clung to them, frozen and soggy. Even their woolen ponchos could not keep out the wetness that fell unceasingly from the sky, or protect their faces from hailstones, or prevent their hands from freezing. They lived on strips of tough beef, cured in the manner of the Mongols by putting the raw meat between the horse and the saddle—the salt sweated from the horse did the curing.

Aurelio's only consolation was that the other gauchos, although they were seasoned, suffered as much as he. More stoically, perhaps. But even custom could not make the change from summer to winter more agreeable.

The second trip he would have avoided, if he could,

but the majordomo was determined to make a gaucho of him as soon as possible. He insisted the boy ride along, if only to round up the stragglers. With Bicho his only mount, Aurelio could not afford to overwork him. It was on the second trip, however, that Aurelio gained himself another horse.

There was a cockfight in one of the towns. Aurelio and the others, their work completed, went to watch. The gambling was as wild as the cockfight. Aurelio found little pleasure in the spectacle, not accustomed enough to brutality and death to accept it as a natural sequence. However, his emotions were sufficiently aroused for him to defend the losing cockerel recklessly, offering Bicho as security for his bet. For some reason, fate was kind to him. His cockerel won! Dazed with disbelief, Aurelio found himself with the choice of a gaucho's string of ponies.

Serafin went with the boy to make sure that he was not swindled. On his advice, Aurelio picked out a strong bay, smaller than Bicho but prettier. The old gaucho assured him that it was the best of the troop. He was right, too, if the loser's face was anything to judge by.

The boy went back to Santa Clara rejoicing, in spite of the rain, the cured beef, and the coldness. He rode the new pony. How beautiful the gray, waterlogged pampa seemed!

The Hunt

Most of the gauchos worked only long enough to earn themselves a few silver pesos. As swiftly as they earned the pesos, they were gone, spent on new clothes, perhaps a new knife, gambling in town, and on other diversions. When the money was gone, the gauchos would go in search of another job. They were too wild and independent to stay at one place for more than a few months. Only a few stayed on, the old ones, like the majordomo, who had done their share of roaming and the temptations of the town no longer appealed to them, and the married ones, who had wives and children living on the estancia.

Sometimes when a gaucho was leaving Santa Clara, he would ask Aurelio if he wanted to go along. The boy always shook his head. He was content to stay where he was, where he had found affection.

Once, when Serafin heard the boy turn down such an invitation, he said, "You can go along if you wish. It's all learning, and you can always come back here when you've had enough, or when you've spent your money."

Aurelio shook his head and smiled. He was not yet gaucho enough to want to roam.

Just as gauchos kept leaving, new ones came. To all Aurelio put the same question about his father. Most of them shook their heads. Once a grizzle-bearded fellow said that he vaguely remembered some such story of a gaucho running off with the daughter of a rich man. But he did not know how the story ended or what had become of either of them. Neither could he recall where first he had heard the story, nor even if it were true.

During the spring branding, the majordomo killed a wild mare. He was in need of a new pair of boots. He made them by pulling off the mare's "socks," from knee to fetlock. The rest of her carcass he left for the carrion birds and wild dogs. It was not until he had finished removing the skin that he discovered a colt that had been running with her. It was little more than a yearling. Serafin pulled it down with his bolas before it could escape. Finding it uninjured, he took it back to Aurelio as a present.

"It's too young to be useful now. You can either keep it or release it as you please," he said.

Aurelio decided to keep it, for he was anxious to make up his troop of horses as quickly as possible. It was a khaki-colored beast, with black points and a small white star on its forehead. He hobbled it, and left it to graze with old Mouse, who was never ridden and continued to be nothing but a bag of bones.

Serafin captured two more colts for the boy, both almost adult and strong enough to be ridden. Again began the bone-jerking, daily battle he had first experienced with Bicho—breaking the colts into submission.

By summer, he had four riding horses, apart from Mouse and the yearling, a small but satisfactory number of silver pesos stowed inside his belt, and the belief that he could truly number himself among the gauchos. This confidence in his skill was due to his age. He was soon to discover that, although he could stay with a bucking horse for at least several minutes, and he was quick at cutting out a cow or calf from the herd, he still had much to learn.

One of the gauchos' favorite pastimes was practicing with bolas. They would take turns throwing them after one another's galloping horses. The majordomo knew by his brightness and boldness of speech that the boy considered himself a man among other men. Partly because he thought a lesson in humility would do Aurelio no harm, and partly to save him from ridicule among gauchos less friendly than those who knew him, he told Aurelio one morning to mount his swiftest horse and see if he could escape the bolas he would swing after him.

The horse he had won at the cockfight, Lucero, was his swiftest. Aurelio sprang to the saddle with a yell. The horse was galloping even before he had his toes in the stirrups. He felt the wind against his eyes, whipping the breath from his throat. It lasted but a second. In an instant, Lucero turned a somersault and Aurelio was flung to the ground, jarring his shoulder horribly. He had traveled no more than fifty yards.

He pulled himself to his feet, then set about untangling the bolas from the bay's hind legs so that he, too, could rise. He was angry with the majordomo for having made a fool of him. He gasped as he pulled the bolas loose, his wrenched shoulder pounding with pain.

Serafín rode up and held out his hand for the bolas.

He saw the flash of anger in the boy's eyes and said im-
placably, "A gaucho would have landed on his feet."

II

One day some Englishmen came to Santa Clara to
speak with Don Jacinto. Aurelio had never seen gringos
before and watched them with undisguised curiosity.

"What do they want with the *patron?*" he asked the
majordomo.

The old man knew, they had come before. "They're
traders in hides and feathers and horsehair. You'll
see. In a few days' time Don Jacinto will send us all
hunting. We'll fill up two or three oxwagons with skins
for the gringos."

So it was. All but a few of the gauchos readied their
best horses, checked to see that their tack was in good
condition, sharpened their knives, and made themselves extra bolas. Hunting and killing were the
gauchos' greatest pleasures. Aurelio had not yet learned
to be as bloodthirsty as they; but he caught the general
excitement, and was as eager for the chase as the
others.

They set off early one morning, before the stars had
faded from the sky. The pampa was still covered in
darkness. Wild shrieks and a horde of pounding hooves
scattered across the pampa. Aurelio's heart thrilled
with fear. He found himself caught up in the midst of
these wild men, knowing instinctively that Bicho was
feeling the same. The bay gelding raced as he had never
raced before. His eyes were wild, his ears flattened
against his skull.

With the dawn, long before they were in sight of

game, the gauchos let fly with their bolas, aiming at
birds who flushed from their nests among the hum-
mocks. Plover and peewits fell, crushed by the spinning
balls. The gauchos leaned from their saddles and
grabbed them up, their mounts not faltering or
slackening in speed. Aurelio marveled at their dexter-
ity. The majordomo's reproof, which still smarted,
suddenly seemed just to him.

When the first flush of excitement faded, the gauchos
drew their mounts to a halt. The ox-drawn carts were
far behind them. The gauchos exchanged horses. Some
stayed on the spot to wait for the wagons, while the
rest went on in search of wild horses, a herd of guanacos, or flock of rheas.

Aurelio was among those who stayed behind. He
chafed at the wasted morning, waiting for the wagons,
knowing that somewhere in the distance his companions were enjoying themselves. At last the wagons
came, the red-and-white oxen strolling doggedly along,
heedless of the driver who poked at them with a long
cane and urged them to go faster. There were three
teams of six oxen each. Aurelio helped to unyoke them
to let them graze, while the men awaited the return
of the hunters.

Eventually they came, their hands and clothes spat-
tered with blood. They had encountered a small herd
of wild horses, which they captured and killed on
the spot. The oxen were yoked again to follow the
gauchos to the place of the killing. When they reached
it Aurelio's eagerness suddenly died.

For an interminable distance the pampa was covered
with the corpses of horses that had died violently. The
earth was soaked red all about them. Already chi-

mangos—pampa hawks—were circling in the wind currents or stalking about on the ground, around the bodies.

The gauchos were unperturbed by the scene, and immediately set to work to skin the animals they had killed. It was a long and wearisome task, there were some three hundred horses lying there. Aurelio was supposed to help, but he stumbled from corpse to corpse, seeing the lifeless eyes staring skyward, the heavy-maned necks stretched out, the jaws drawn back in a frozen whinny of terror and pain. They haunted him. He could not bring himself to lay a hand on them, let alone hack off their tails.

The next day the gauchos fell upon a flock of rheas. Aurelio was among them this time. He learned why the gauchos referred to this bird as the most "gaucho" of all the pampa dwellers. In astuteness, it was next to the gaucho himself, and no easy prey to catch. Just as the hunter was within reach of it and about to swing his bolas, the rhea would twist back on its tracks with such rapidity that, before the gaucho realized it, the rhea was behind the horse. While the gaucho checked his mount's mad career and turned about, the rhea made good its escape. The rhea was the swiftest of creatures, capable of outrunning the freshest horse, and all the gaucho's skill, cunning, and patience were needed to entrap it.

About seventy birds were brought down that morning; the others escaped. Aurelio did nothing but chase halfheartedly, swinging the bolas but not releasing it from his grasp. There was more blood and plenty of feathers for women's hats, which would fetch a good price in the city.

The hunters scoured the pampa for fifteen days before setting a homeward course. The three big wagons were heavy with multicolored hides, big bundles of horsehair, and stacks of soft, plumy feathers. The men were contented, the lust to kill gone out of them. With some thousand horses dead on the pampa behind them, they were still able to sing with all sincerity, "My horse was my life, my welfare, my only treasure."

The majordomo rode alongside Aurelio. He knew of the boy's unhappiness without needing to inquire. He waited for Aurelio to speak, giving him a chance to pour out the sickness that was in him. Aurelio said nothing. He had come to the pampa wanting to be a gaucho. But the boy who had delighted to gaze upon the flower gardens in rich men's houses could not stomach the sight of slaughter.

For hours they rode side by side, Serafin seemingly asleep on his pony. Aurelio gazed steadfastly ahead and jabbed at his mount with his heels whenever memories could not be kept at bay. The majordomo gave up. He sighed, spurred his horse forward, and took up his position at the head of the column. But three words he said to Aurelio before he left him, to let him know that he sympathized and understood without condoning.

"Get hard, boy."

III

Don Jacinto was well pleased with the results of the gauchos' labors. On the day that the gringos returned to Santa Clara to discuss prices, he told the majordomo to arrange a fiesta. Cows and a few sheep were killed for the barbecue. The married men rode in haste for their wives and children. Some of the others went in search of their sweethearts to bring them to the dance that was scheduled for the evening.

The gauchos engaged in equestrian sports, which were, for the most part, both primitive and dangerous. Aurelio was unable to partake; he would have assuredly been killed. But there were horse races in which he dared to match his Lucero against the others. He found, though, that swiftness was not enough, and that trickery was not only permitted but expected. Lucero came in last in every race. Again it was evident that, for all he could judge himself a good rider by city standards, Aurelio was still only a beginner among the gauchos.

The roasted meats were attacked with gusto, and chunks were thrown generously to the dogs that hung around. In the afternoon, a turgid silence fell over the men and the dogs and the horses, all tired and replete. Aurelio could not doze easily, in spite of the good meat he had eaten and the wine he had drunk.

Nearby a gaucho was softly singing the ballad, "My horse was my life, my welfare, my only treasure." It brought back vividly all that he was trying to forget of the last few weeks. He had seen Don Jacinto and the Englishmen haggling the whole morning over the price for the skins and feathers, while on the pampa the hawks and wild dogs would still be gorging on the carcasses. One day, he supposed, a storm would wash the blood away.

Land of Mists

The following autumn, the majordomo told Aurelio that he was leaving the estancia to go on a cattle drive that would take three months to complete.

"Don Jacinto has some land to the south, a miserable country for sure. It's overrun with cattle, some branded and some not. We only go down there once every three or four years to brand the new stock, kill off the diseased ones, and choose the best of the bunch to take to the city. Only six of us are going, so it will be hard work. If you want to come along, you're welcome."

Aurelio was beginning to tire of Santa Clara at last. The work was routine now that he could perform it reasonably well. This sounded like an adventure and would give him a chance to see a bit of the world.

"Don't deceive yourself," warned the old gaucho. "It's not country like this. It's along the coast. There's hardly any grass, it's all sand—hills of it as far as the eye can see, which isn't far, for sure. Thick mists cover the land the best part of the year. And the cattle aren't like the ones you know. They're wild, with monstrous horns and devilish natures. What with the sand dunes and the mist, you can hardly see them until they're on top of you. And it's a miserable place to die."

"I'm not afraid," replied Aurelio.

"No, I don't suppose you are. But remember, I've

warned you. It's no place for novices. You can come along, but you'd better leave the big cattle alone. There'll be enough for you to do, helping with the branding and the calf-cutting."

The six gauchos and Aurelio set out from the estancia three days later. Aurelio left Mouse behind on this trip, and took only Bicho, Lucero, and the two new geldings. Contrary to custom, none of the men seemed very cheerful at the outset of the journey. They rode in silence with fixed, implacable expressions. The only sound was the discordant jangling induced by the movements of the six bell mares.

"What's the matter?" Aurelio asked Serafin. "Are we going to a funeral?"

"Perhaps. I told you it's a miserable place. The only beings that inhabit it are ghosts and bad spirits. You can hear them moaniug and howling at night and even during the day. And sometimes, in the night, you can feel them touching your face."

II

The gaucho had not exaggerated his description of the country into which they eventually rode. The seven riders huddled up in their ponchos and pulled down the brims of their hats. Even Aurelio, in spite of his boyish enthusiasm, felt the oppressiveness of the atmosphere and grew as silent as the rest. It had taken them three weeks to come down to this God-forsaken coastland. The horses trod it unwillingly. The good pampa grass was left behind, here there was only gorse and reeds and a dry, salty grass that was strange to their palates.

The wind blew in from the sea, and the air was thick with salt and dampness. Aurelio felt as clammy and uncomfortable as if he had ridden for days through a rainstorm. The sound of the sea, sighing in the distance, disturbed his imagination. Were these the spirits of which the majordomo spoke, already acknowledging their advent?

In the early mornings, the sun shone, like an orange ball through the mists. It was never seen in its entirety, but as a blurred stain above them. The horses expressed their dislike for the terrain by blowing often through their nostrils. Their eyes were white-ringed, and their ears flattened aganst their skulls.

When it was necessary to stop and make camp, none of the horses wandered far from the men. They kept within sight of the fire, bulky shadows on the rim of the flickering light, and the bells of the mares sounded hollowly in the gloomy darkness. The gauchos drew close and hardly spoke. All were listening for unexpected sounds. There was not one who doubted the existence of malevolent spirits. Now and again, one of them would pull out a medallion worn on a chain around his neck, kiss it, and mutter a short prayer. They slept with their heads pointed in the direction in which they were traveling, for in the gray, blurred light of day, the countryside had no distinguishing marks.

Once they came onto the beach, a long wilderness, with driftwood and seaweed blackening the waves as they ran up to the sand. The horses trod fearfully. Aurelio was spellbound by his first sight of the gray sea. In a way, it was like the pampa, unchanging and endless, the only difference being that the sea was alive, its surface in constant turmoil, and the waves came up like crested, tossing horses, as savage and as unrestrained.

The sea disappeared into the misty distance. Aurelio,

alone on the sand with his horse—the others had ridden ahead, and left him to his gazing—was overwhelmed by a sensation of emptiness and was suddenly afraid. He jerked his horse around and set him at a gallop after the others. He was glad when they left the beach to follow a rough trail which wound through sand dunes, and led them eventually to a rancho, inhabited by a shepherd and his wife. There they stopped for the night, at the shepherd's insistence. So rarely did he see strangers, he could not let them ride by.

Aurelio was glad to be inside a house again. He welcomed the heat of the log fire, and the light it gave flickeringly to the room. It was a big room, with several dogs sharing the floor space that was alloted to them for sleeping. The shepherd butchered a sheep, and his wife attended to the cooking of it. The gauchos for once grew voluble as they asked questions of the shepherd or replied to those put by their hosts.

On the following day, they reached their destination, a deserted ranch house. The gauchos gave it life when they threw down their belongings and set about stirring up a fire. The walls were damp and the roof was broken in places, letting in the mist through the rafters. The horses were put to graze; the sheep the shepherd had presented to them was killed and jabbed on the spit in the fireplace. While they ate, the majordomo outlined the work that was expected of them.

Aurelio discovered that he was, indeed, only to help with the branding and calf-cutting. He now considered them almost a child's job; he was not very pleased. He had worked hard with his horses all summer, teaching them the tricks they needed to know. Now he wanted an opportunity to try out both their skill and his own.

These wild cattle represented a challenge, and, it seemed, he would not have the opportunity to meet it.

Serafin read the boy's thoughts. As they settled down to sleep on their sheepskin saddles, he admonished him. "Leave the bulls and the big cows alone."

III

For several days Aurelio worked with efficiency but impatience at his allocated job. He was ready with the branding irons and the cutting knife whenever a calf was brought. He envied the gauchos who returned to the base every two or three hours to change horses and to speak briefly of the the cattle they hunted.

"Every one is possessed of a devil," said a gaucho. He showed the boy the great gash across his mount's breast where a horn had gouged into it. "My best horse, too."

Once, such evidence might have deterred Aurelio from attempting his skill with wild cattle. But he had grown fearless as his confidence increased, and considered that the accident was due to bad luck, or the fact that working in the mist made things difficult. He was certain that with Bicho or Lucero to aid him, he could easily cut out the calves from the herd and, afterward, try his skill with something bigger. He said nothing to the majordomo.

At the end of a week the majordomo called a rest. In the old corral that had been built near the house some twenty years earlier, there were already more than sixty bullocks. Aurelio went to look at them and found them inferior beasts, most of their weight being in the huge horns they carried. They were skeleton-thin and wiry. He had never seen such animals on the pampa, where the grass and flowers and alfalfa were in abundance, making the animals grow fat and lethargic. He could not imagine why Don Jacinto troubled with them. And these were the best of the herd! He was curious to know what the others looked like.

As it was a day of rest, each man busied himself as he chose, some mending broken harnesses, some passing round the maté pot and talking desultorily. Aurelio decided to take a horse and wander about on his own, to see if he could find some of the dangerous bulls that the gauchos spoke of, and which, so far, he had not seen. He was riding Bicho.

The boy had grown accustomed to the strange climate, with its mists that rarely lifted, its dampness, and the salt that clung to his skin. Still the atmosphere perturbed him, and he longed for the fresh winds of the pampa and its skies of blue and white.

It was pleasant to be alone for a while. A sense of excitement, mingled almost with dread, tingled through him. Aurelio knew in his heart, without actually admitting it, that if he encountered any of the wild cattle, he would try out his skill. He did not intend to actually look for them. He touched the bolas that was wound about his waist, growing in confidence at the feel of it. If he found them. . . .

Silence wrapped itself about him. He could hardly even hear the sound of Bicho's hooves, so thick was the ground with wind-blown sand. He rode with the reins slack. Bicho grazed as he wandered along, snatching at the salty grass with distaste but hunger. Now and again the mist lifted, and he could see for quite a distance. At other times, it seemed to drop like a blanket over everything, and he was aware only of the sand dunes.

Then, when least he expected it, he came across a whole bunch of the wild cattle, grazing in a hollow. He jerked his horse to a stop to gaze at them. As he looked from one to another, he realized that the sixty in the corral were in reality the best of the lot. These were the most revolting and monstrous animals he had ever seen, belonging indeed to this nightmare country. Their bodies were covered with maggot-ridden sores; their horns were deformed and grew into their eyes; some dragged broken limbs, and all were as gaunt as empty wine skins. Even the freshblooded calves could not escape the curse of their birthplace. They were pitiful, rickety beasts, abandoned to the harshness of nature.

All at once—hardly more than a hundred paces away —a bulky shadow appeared from behind a sand dune. By the wide expanse of horn, surely too heavy for that paper-thin body to support, Aurelio had no doubt about his adversary. For a moment, he was taken aback, so suddenly had the beast appeared. Then he saw how he tore at the ground with his hoof, and lowered the impossibly long horns with a menacing twist.

Aurelio began to back Bicho away. Then he remembered his intentions, and hurriedly pulled the bolas into his hand. The bull advanced imperceptibly, not decided yet whether or not to attack. Aurelio recalled his lessons, and drew Bicho away. The bull was close, dangerously so, and gave him no room for maneuvers.

Bicho's head-tossing retreat decided the bull. With another shake of his prehistoric horns, the bull came after the horse and rider. Giving a yell, Aurelio dug his heels in the pony's flanks, and Bicho fled, the bull in close pursuit. Aurelio zigzagged as much as the dunes would let him, until the bull fell off the boy's trail. Then Aurelio turned around, ready to chase the bull in his turn.

But the bull had no fear. Instead of racing away from his pursuer, he whirled in his tracks and came after Aurelio again. The boy was disconcerted by the bull's swiftness and unexpected behavior. Bicho's own instinct of self-preservation saved them. The bay gelding hastily side-stepped the charging animal, and the left horn missed him by inches. Again the bull turned. He was fast in spite of his top-heavy horns, and Aurelio had no time to swing the bola with any effect in the short space and time available to him.

He pulled the horse around and spurred him away, needing more space. But he had forgotten the difficult terrain. This was no flat grassland for easy running and leisurely maneuvers. Bicho lost ground as his hooves sank into the sandy earth. He slipped against a sand dune and almost floundered.

The bull was upon them as Aurelio jerked his pony up. He saw the brindle head and the blood-red eyes. Bicho struggled, and Aurelio felt the gelding being lifted beneath him.

The horse screamed as Aurelio flung himself from the saddle, landing on the side of the dune. In the same second, he was aware of the sand giving softly under his feet, the rank smell of his fear-sweating horse, and the grunts of the savage bull. Then a heavy weight collapsed on top of him. The gray day turned black.

The Parting

When Aurelio opened his eyes, he thought he was dreaming. He was in a room illuminated by firelight, and he could vaguely make out the shadow of the roof with its smoke-blackened beams, the smudged uneven walls, and the figure of a shawl-shrouded woman sitting near him. It was Tia Luisa, and all that was in his memory had been a dream.

He went to sit up and call to her, but the call became a gasp of pain. He fell back again on the sheepskins. The beams and the walls spun. The woman had risen to her feet and, when she no longer spun with her surroundings, Aurelio realized that she was not Tia Luisa at all, though her face was familiar.

"Lie still," came the soft command.

Weakly, Aurelio asked, "Where am I? What's happened?"

"Don't you remember?"

Slowly, Aurelio forced his memory. "You're the shepherd's wife . . . bull attacked me . . . my horse! What happened to my horse?"

"It's dead, and so is the horse of the majordomo. He saved you, or you'd be dead too."

Aurelio moved his head restlessly. He could remember nothing more than Bicho's terrible scream, the soft sand and the snorting bull. How did the majordomo come to be mixed up in it?

"Don't move," cautioned the woman. "You've crushed most of your ribs, so be still."

There was nothing else the boy could do. The slight breath he took made him dizzy with pain. He was strapped from his chin to his waist in sheepskins and any movement was impossible. He closed his eyes and let the pain sweep over him. Later, he was aware of the woman trying to push some liquid between his lips.

"It's a pain-killing herb I've brewed," she explained as she saw his eyes open. "Swallow."

Aurelio obeyed. Soon he was drifting into a world of dreams again. He dreamed of Tia Luisa and green patios, the majordomo, and his screaming horse.

How long he lived in this shadowy world of pain and dreams, Aurelio did not know. One day, he came out of it. Though the pain was still there, it was bearable. He watched the woman going about her work in the house, tending the fire and the meals. Bent over her sewing in the afternoons, she made him think of Tia Luisa. She attended him with gentleness in spite of the abruptness of her speech.

Now and again, a gaucho would come to see how the boy was progressing. The majordomo never came, and Aurelio was too ashamed to ask for him.

One day, he demanded of a gaucho, "What happened? Tell me! I don't remember anything."

"I only know what the majordomo told us," said the gaucho. "He followed you because he guessed what you were up to, but he lost you in the mist. It wasn't until he heard your horse screaming that he discovered you again. You were crushed beneath the dying horse.

He drove at the bull, but the savage was mad with lust and wouldn't leave your horse alone. Serafin grabbed the bull by the tail, to pull him off balance. Then the bull went for him too. Serafin drew the bull away, chasing around the sand dunes."

The gaucho paused, and then cried, "It was all the fault of the accursed mist! The bull disappeared. Although Serafin searched for him, the bull had vanished like a spirit in the night."

"Then what happened?" asked Aurelio, almost fearfully, the nightmare memory of the monstrous bull returning.

"The old man went back to free you from your dead horse. While he was doing that, the bull was suddenly in front of him again, with murder in his eyes. Serafin's horse shied away in fear, and the bull went after him. The horse's legs got tangled in the reins, and when he fell the bull finished him off. The majordomo carried you back to the camp. Then we brought you here to be looked after by the shepherd's wife."

"And the bull?" said Aurelio.

"The majordomo took another horse and went in search of him. He was angry, angrier than I've ever seen him. It was his favorite horse that he lost. When he came back half the day had gone by, and we were beginning to be afraid for him."

The gaucho stopped for a moment, then he continued almost wonderingly. "He'd found the bull and broken his neck with his own hands. We couldn't believe it until we went to see. But it was true. The bull lay there with his head twisted. There wasn't a drop of blood on him, except from the horses."

II

While Aurelio lay helplessly on his back, the days passing slowly and the nights pain-filled, he often thought of the majordomo and his manner of killing the bull. His vivid imagination pictured the scene; the gray-bearded old gaucho with his hands on the bull's horns, dragging it down and down in his rage until, with a final jerk, it was subjugated forever. The dead horse had been his pride and joy. He had loved it as only a man can when he has neither wife, nor children, nor brothers.

Worse than the pain of his broken ribs, was the realization that Serafin would probably never forgive him for his disobedience and for unwittingly causing the death of his horse. The majordomo never came to the shepherd's house, and Aurelio was heavyhearted. His fondness for the man was second only to the love he had borne for Tia Luisa.

His foolishness had cost him the old man's respect and affection as well as the life of his own horse. He had been fond of Bicho. The boy recalled the time he had broken the bay gelding in the corral at Santa Clara and how the majordomo had encouraged him. Tears came to his eyes. This was indeed an accursed land that, in the same hour, had robbed him of both friend and pony.

While the boy pondered and grieved in the shepherd's home, the gauchos finished their work with the wild cattle. They had some four hundred animals to drive back to the estancia, and they were glad to go. Winter was approaching. The mists were growing heavier and the nights were freezing.

On the last day, the majordomo finally came to see Aurelio. He made no mention of the boy's accident, except to say in his usual undemonstrative manner, "If you're well enough to sit on a horse you'd better come with us."

Nothing more would Aurelio have desired. But he was hardly able to lift himself from the sheepskin rug on which he lay. He could never have endured the long journey back to the pampa.

"I can't," he replied.

"Then we shall have to go without you. The work's finished, and we can't stay here any longer. When you're better you'll be able to find your own way back . . . unless you decide you like it down here. Ride northward, and one day you'll reach the pampa."

Aurelio nodded, afraid to speak. He knew his voice would come out in a sob.

"Your horses are outside," added the other.

Aurelio nodded again.

"Well," said Serafin. There was a silence between them while they stared at each other. "Well," he said again, "we're off."

"Go with God," Aurelio forced himself to reply.

The majordomo walked over to the door. He stopped in the entrance and looked back at Aurelio.

"And when you're better . . . don't go playing 'gaucho' any more. You can't afford to crack your ribs a second time."

"What must I do then?"

This time the sob escaped and, although he pretended not to hear it, the old gaucho relented a little.

"There's a legend hereabouts. The man who can find and ride the sand stallion will be the most 'gaucho' of them all. You'd better look for him. Whether he exists or not, I don't know." He grinned at the boy and added, "But at least he won't have horns."

And then he was gone. Aurelio heard his yell and the startled pounding of his horse's hooves. He listened to their rhythmic movement over the earth until they grew fainter and fainter, and finally disappeared. Aurelio felt a great emptiness. The pain of emptiness was greater than any caused by his broken ribs.

Later, when the woman came to ask the boy if he were hungry, he turned his face to the wall so that she could not see his tear-stained cheeks.

The Sand Stallion

The boy knew Serafin had spoken in jest when he told him to find the stand stallion. Having nothing to do but lie on the ground and think, however, the idea soon took hold of his imagination. He asked the shepherd if he knew of the legend.

"The sand stallion?" said the shepherd. "Yes, I've heard of him. He's a white stallion that's supposed to live in these parts. It must be just a legend. I've never seen him."

"How old is the legend?" Aurelio wanted to know.

The shepherd shrugged his shoulders. "It must have started six or seven years ago. The gauchos who come down here began saying they had seen a beautiful white stallion. Whenever they chased him, he always disappeared into the sea. That's the legend of the stallion. To my mind, it was the mist that deceived them."

"Is that all?" said Aurelio. It seemed very little.

The shepherd hesitated and then continued, "Once, when I'd been laughing at the gauchos for chasing after this will-o'-the-wisp, they took me with them to where they'd last seen it—a long distance off, in an inlet where the sea comes up to a river. There's a long stretch of narrow beach there. The hard sand near the water's edge was all churned up with the hoofprints of a galloping horse. The rest of the beach was full of the prints of the gauchos' horses, but none of them had come down to the water's edge. You could see that the prints were distinct from the rest—big ones."

"Has Serafin ever seen him?"

"Old Serafin? So he says. That old one sees many things that others don't see, so who's to know whether it's true or not? If anyone could catch the sand stallion, he could. Yet he never has."

Aurelio had to acknowledge the truth of this last statement. All the same, he fell to musing over what the shepherd had told him.

"And where is this beach where the stallion was seen going into the water?"

"You must ride southeast for at least half a day. Follow the coast, and eventually you'll come to the river's mouth. There you'll find the beach."

"But couldn't the horse swim across the river?"

"No. It's far too wide there. It's more like a big bay. To find the river by following the beach would take another afternoon's riding. A horse entering the water there would surely be drowned. It's only a tale."

Aurelio wondered. One thing he was determined to do, legend or not; he would search for the sand stallion. If he did find him, he would not return to the pampa until he had caught and tamed him. Then he would take him back to Santa Clara as a gift for the major-domo.

II

It was almost spring before Aurelio was strong enough to get up on a horse again. He had grown considerably and was less thin than before. The shepherd's wife had coddled him with stews and roasts, which he had been unable to work off by physical energy. His ribs were still strapped up in the woman's primitive bandages, and he could not move with ease. He was sick of his enforced idleness in the shepherd's house. Like a captive bird, he longed for freedom.

The landscape was gray. The autumn mists had become thick Atlantic fogs, which the strong winds from the coast could hardly move. It often rained. Aurelio wondered if the sun ever shone on this God-forsaken part of the world.

His horses were wild and almost uncontrollable. They had spent all the time of Aurelio's illness in hobbled freedom, with no man to molest them. It took him a whole morning to find all of them. They had wandered far in search of the mean fodder the land provided. Had they not been hobbled, it would have been a difficult task to catch them. He longed for old Mouse, incapable of the smallest buck or twist. His ribs were in no condition to endure the shaking that the colts would give them.

When he told the shepherd of his intention to search for the sand stallion, the man stared at him incredulously.

"You must be mad!" he exclaimed. "It might take you months to even catch a glimpse of him—assuming that he exists. Meanwhile you'll freeze and die. I doubt that you're accustomed to such weather as this."

"I can accustom myself to anything," replied Aurelio, his self-confidence fully restored. "I've taken advantage of your hospitality for long enough. Now I must go."

"Then go back to the pampa. Don't be a fool!"

"Not until I've found the stallion. When I return to the pampa, I intend to take him with me."

"Fool!" reiterated the shepherd. "But do as you please."

The woman gave him a wool-lined jacket to wear under his poncho; and the man, a hunk of cured beef.

"The hunting is poor here," he said. "You'll go back to the pampa a lot thinner than you are now."

Aurelio thanked them again for their kindness. Riding Lucero, he was on his way. His heart was light in spite of the wind-blown rain that sprayed finely into his face. Instinct told him that the stallion existed and that he would find him.

He rode as the shepherd had directed him. As he neared the sea, the rain had a salty flavor and was icy on his cheeks. His horses went forward with lowered heads. At first, the rain had run off them in rivulets. Now, the horses were so soaked that the rain clung to their hair, grown thick in the many months that they had dwelt in this cold, unfriendly land.

By the time he reached the coast, Aurelio's whole body ached. He knew that for that day at least he could go no further. He searched about for shelter, which was only to be had from a copse of westerly-inclined gorse bushes. He hobbled the horses, made himself as comfortable as possible—which was very little— and pulled from his saddlebag the cured beef. As the shepherd had warned him, there was nothing to hunt.

By nightfall, he wished he had listened to the shepherd and not set out on such a journey. He was cold and pain-filled and miserable. The sound of the sea reminded him of the spirits that terrified the gauchos. It was too damp to light a fire, even had he possessed the energy to search for fuel. He spent the best part of the long, cold night in wakefulness. Even the thought of capturing the legendary stallion could not comfort him.

The next morning he felt more cheerful. The fog had lifted considerably, although the skies were still gloomy, giving the impression that the landscape was as gray as they were. At least he could see where he was going, and he felt less oppressed by the atmosphere. The sea was a stormy black. The waves crashed onto the beach with a fury that startled the boy.

Surely no horse, however powerful, could swim through that sea and survive. He stared keenly into the distance. The mist was heavy over the sea and little was visible beyond a short distance. The waves seemed to meet the fog, and beyond was the end of the world, nothingness.

Aurelio saddled a different horse and decided to find the river's mouth. He followed the beach. At times, he was almost blown off the animal's back by the fierce gusts of wind that had gathered speed and fury out in the mid-Atlantic. They came rushing into the coast, flattening everything in their path. The noise of the sea and the rushing wind began to unnerve the boy, used to the silence of the pampa, broken only by sweet birdsong in the daytime.

He tried to sing, recalling one or two ballads he had heard when they were driving cattle. He made up his own phrases when he could not remember the correct ones. The wind whipped the words out of his mouth, and he could not even hear them. So he gave up singing and rode on in dour silence.

Eventually, he came to what appeared to be the

mouth of the river. A torrent of ice-cold water rushed to meet the waves. Where they met, the water was brown and murky. It lashed and writhed. The land was marshy and thick with rushes, which stood up fine and straight in spite of the wind. To find shelter, he had to go inland a way. He was luckier than in his previous quest. He found a hollow underneath a jutting, centuries-old sandbank. The wind and the sea spray could not enter, and there he felt almost comfortable.

The hollow became his base. He spent the next few days collecting driftwood, which he hoped would eventually dry enough for burning. He was able to capture a couple of ducks quite easily, so unused were they to creatures other than themselves in that deserted terrain. They were almost curious about him, allowing him to approach, grab them, and cut their throats, all within a matter of seconds.

He allowed the horses to roam in search of grazing. As he finished hobbling them and sent them off with a whack on the rump, he suddenly wished that one of them were a mare. A mare would have been good bait for the stallion. Still, perhaps even the smell of the geldings would be enough to attract him, for surely there were no other horses in this part of the world. Curiosity would bring him, assuming that he was flesh and not just a spirit.

III

Dawn never came until the morning was already advanced. Daylight lasted but a few hours. Every day Aurelio used those precious hours to search the beach and surrounding countryside for hoofprints. The rest of the time he spent huddled up in his poncho, sleeping as much as he could to forget his discomfort, almost in hibernation.

Often he was ready to give up his quest, so hopeless did it seem and so miserable was he. But he remembered what he owed to the majordomo, and stayed on. There was nowhere to go, anyway, unless he returned to Santa Clara.

The loneliness made his imagination acute. He thought he could see a white stallion among the mists and fogs. But he was accustomed to seeing mirages on the pampa and knew when his eyes were deceiving him. But surely his ears could not deceive him also?

He awoke one morning to the sound of excitement among the horses, who never strayed far from the fireside at night. There were grunts and whinnies and the striking of hooves on the ground. Had the stallion come at last to visit them? Surely there was no other explanation.

Swiftly but with caution, Aurelio arose and went in search of the horses. The fog was there as usual, cutting visibility down almost to nil, and making every shape strange and unearthly. As the vague outlines of the horses came into view, he counted them. One over to the right, standing still and watchful; the bay, too, with a similar stance. Where was the little dun with the black legs? In a moment, Aurelio caught sight of him. He, too, was motionless, staring with pricked ears into the mist-bound distance. The boy drew near, and saw that the dun was trembling.

In the next second, a big shape reared out of the mist. There was the stallion, whiter—far whiter—than the mist. His muscles bulged and his hooves struck the ground haughtily; his blood-red eyes made Aurelio think of the bull. Instantly, the stallion was gone. Aurelio was left wondering if he had really seen the stallion or only dreamed him.

No, the reaction of his ponies proved that it was no dream. In spite of his awesome spiritlike appearance, in spite of his incredible whiteness and blood-red eyes, the stallion was flesh. Therefore, he could be caught and tamed.

In a moment, Aurelio had the hobbles off the dun and was on his back, following the direction taken by the stallion. There was no sight of him. But the hoofprints in the damp, sandy earth were deep and distinct and easy to follow. They led, exactly as in the legend, down to the beach as far as the water's edge.

When he got there, there was no sight of the stallion. The rough waves were already beginning to wash at the hoofprints and erase them.

An Outlaw's Story

Aurelio watched the waves creep up on the hoofprints.
He was almost mesmerized by their unceasing, relentless motion. Then he stared into the fog-bound sea, wondering how it was that the stallion could disappear into it and not be drowned. He knew, now that he had seen the animal, that he was flesh and blood. He could not vanish into the sea without some practical explanation.

Nothing but the fog, unmoving and gray, touched the water. Aurelio shivered as the wind from the Atlantic blew in strongly. The dun grew restless and pawed the sand. The wind tangled the horse's mane and blew its black hairs against the boy's face as he leaned forward, trying to peer through the fog.

He had to admit that the stallion had defeated him, unless he could discover the reason for his ability to vanish in such a spiritlike manner. The only way to discover it was by following him into the sea. Aurelio shuddered. The almost black water was not inviting, and looked treacherous. He knew how to swim, for his main delight in the summer weather had been bathing in the river near his home. There was a great difference, however, between that slow, marshy water and this turbulent darkness that swept over the sand, reaching for his pony's hooves.

He would die of cold in that water or be swept

away. But the same could be said of the stallion. A horse could resist only for so long before growing tired and cold. Yet the stallion had come from the water and returned to it for at least six years, if he were to believe the shepherd.

Hesitating no longer, Aurelio urged the pony into the water. Having come so far to find the stallion, he could not lose him now. With courage he would solve the riddle, of this he was sure. He forced the dun against his will into the waves and gritted his teeth against the unbearable coldness of the water. His lessons in endurance proved not to be in vain.

The pony struggled and resisted until, caught from behind by the waves that receded swiftly from the shore, he was forced to go on. With the courage of his race and the urgings of his master, he struck out toward the gray horizon, plunging and snorting, his eyes wild with fright.

Aurelio clung to the pony's mane with his hands, and to his back with his knees. Never had he welded himself so closely to a horse as now. The water rose up to the gelding's withers, and such a coldness came over the boy that soon he was unable to feel his legs at all, nor the body of the pony. He was swept from the dun's back and grabbed at his neck fiercely, his fingers locked together, frozen in that position.

He lost all count of time and direction, dragged through the sea by the struggling horse. For a while, he must have lost consciousness too. He knew that they were in the grip of a strong current, dragging them he knew not where. *To the stallion!* he thought. *To the stallion!* Then the waves no longer crashed over his head. He thought of nothing.

His next awareness came when the dun was no longer swimming, and seemed to have firm ground under his hooves once more. Aurelio was unable to release his fingers from their frozen grasp. He floated beside the pony until, at last, he could get a leg across his back again. Thus he remained, half on the pony and half in the water. The waves suddenly receded, and the dun brought him to shore.

The gelding stood still with drooping head, too exhausted even to shake the water from his body. Aurelio slipped from his back, his fingers loosened at last, and fell unconscious to the ground.

II

Aurelio came to his senses, aware of warmth and dryness, and a darkness that was broken by the flickering light of a fire. At first he thought he was in the shepherd's hut. He was lying on a sheepskin rug, a thick poncho over him. The warmth of the two combined almost lulled him back into slumber. He was thoroughly battered by his sojourn in the sea, and had no energy for anything.

His eyes closed. But they opened again sharply as a shadow fell over him. It was a gaucho, no doubt the owner of the place in which he rested. His beard was gray and his hair came down to his shoulders.

"Where am I?" said Aurelio.

"In your house," replied the gaucho, which was his way of offering the boy his hospitality.

"But where did you find me?"

"I saw your horse and looked for you."

"But where is this place? I never saw a homestead

in these parts, except for the shepherd's, and that's a good journey from here."

"I know him. No, you're nowhere near the shepherd's home, nor are you anywhere that you could imagine, though I can guess how you got here."

The gaucho went over to the fire. A kettle hung over its flames, gushing a volley of steam. Aurelio sat up, pulled the poncho around him, and watched in silence while his host prepared a pot of maté. He was even more puzzled by the man's last words.

He was aware again of the sound of the sea, loud and unceasing. It made him think that he must still be somewhere along the shore. The hut was very tiny. Aurelio was obviously lying on the gaucho's bed.

The gaucho brought the maté over to the boy and squatted down beside him. They shared it between them in silence. Aurelio's head was spinning with questions, so many that he did not know where to begin. His companion's expression suggested that he was not thinking of anything at all.

But at last the gaucho spoke. His words, quiet and unexpected, were startling.

"You're on an island, an island that's not very far away from the beach. On a clear day it can be plainly seen. But on a day like this, no one would ever guess its existence. If you see it from a distance, the island looks as though it's part of the mainland. The fact is, this part of the world is the most deserted on God's earth. No one ever comes this way. Should they come, they don't stay long enough to discover its secrets."

"But the shepherd?" broke in Aurelio.

"The shepherd has only been in these parts once, and it was on a day as gray as this one. He thinks I live inland. No one knows about this little rancho of mine, except you and the stallion."

"The stallion?"

"Yes. The one you were undoubtedly chasing. What else would have caused you to launch yourself into the sea like a madman? Why else would you be in these parts?"

Aurelio explained what had happened. His companion listened, nodding his head, not once interrupting.

"You have courage at least," was his only comment when the boy had finished.

"And the stallion?" said Aurelio eagerly. "Was I right? Did I follow him here? Is this where he comes?"

"And if it is?"

"Well. . . ." He paused as a thought suddenly struck him. "I suppose he belongs to you."

The gaucho shook his head. "We share the island. He doesn't bother me, and I don't bother him."

"You mean you've never tried to catch him?" The incredulity in his voice amused the gaucho.

"Why should I? We're a pair of recluses who happen to have found refuge from the world in the same place. It may not be the most comfortable or the most accommodating, but neither of us wanted to be disturbed by men. Until your arrival, this is about the only place that men have never ventured to come."

The gaucho brewed another pot of maté. When he squatted down beside the mystified boy, he told him one of the strangest stories Aurelio had ever heard—one that he had least expected to hear in, of all places, the hermit's hut.

"I'm an outlaw," he began, "a deserter from the

army. You don't know what the army's like, and I
hope you never will. A long time ago, I was as free as
any man under the sun. One day, for a reason I don't
even remember now, I got into a fight with another
gaucho. I was a hot-blooded fellow in those days, and
wouldn't take an insult from anybody. He was a bad
one. He would rather use a knife than words to settle
his quarrels. It's wrong to start a fight. But if a man
pulls a knife on you, what can you do? Without ever
meaning to, I killed him. There were plenty of wit-
nesses to prove that it was in self-defense."

He snorted, angry at the memory of that day long
ago. "It was obvious that the army was short of men,
which doesn't surprise me. No one in his right senses
would volunteer. The judge didn't even listen to my
argument. Twenty-five years of army service was the
sentence, and a staking besides. I would have killed
that judge with pleasure."

The gaucho rambled on for a long time about his
life in the army, full of woes and injustice, hunger
and pain. Aurelio listened with his eyes shut. He had
snuggled back under the poncho, and felt warm and
dreamy. The sea roared outside the hut, but he hardly
heard it. The voice of the recluse, silent for too long to
be anything less than voluble, was lulling him slowly
to sleep.

Was it instinct that suddenly jerked him into wakefulness, that made him, all at once, take notice? The
gaucho brought another gaucho into his story, whose
woes were even greater than his own. He was a young
man, at least twenty years the storyteller's junior, who
was dragged into the outpost more dead than alive. He
had suffered at the hands of a justice of peace, much

as had the narrator of his story.

"They said he was a criminal. All gauchos are criminals, even before they have committed a crime. This gaucho was supposed to have kidnapped the daughter of a rich man and murdered her. It was just an excuse to bring the army up to strength. The Indians were a lot stronger than we were."

"What happened to him?" asked Aurelio, an eager listener once more.

"I had been wounded in a battle against the Indians, which kept me around the fort for a while. I looked after him until he was able to look after himself. Soon we became companions. Mind you, he made himself popular with most of the men. He was a bit of a poet and, heaven knows, we all needed a few songs to cheer us up. We were desperate men, with hardly a meal a day. Even the horses starved.

"Anyway, he was determined to escape just as soon as he could stand on his feet. I held him back for a while—he would never have succeeded otherwise. Then we decided to escape together. There was only one place we could go until our desertion would be forgotten, and that was to the Indians."

The gaucho paused, remembering too vividly the past that this boy had unexpectedly caused him to conjure up.

"Go on," said Aurelio impatiently. "What happened next?"

"Oh, we escaped. The Indians accepted us in their way, which wasn't friendly. But at least they allowed us to live on their lands, which was all we wanted. At least, it was all I wanted. I had no one to go back to. It was all the same to me if I lived in one place or another. But for my companion, it was different.

"The woman he was supposed to have kidnapped was his wife. They had run away together and married in spite of her father, who had tried to prevent them. But she died, after giving birth to a son. Only a few days afterward, he was captured by the men the girl's father had paid to search for them. The pair had been on the run the whole of the short time they were married, trying to escape their pursuers. Perhaps if they hadn't stopped at that town they might eventually have escaped them.

"The girl's father was very rich, a powerful man. When he learned that his daughter was dead, his rage was insatiable. My friend refused to tell him where the baby was. Whether the old man ever found out, I wouldn't know. You see, the gaucho had to get back to find his son, regardless of the danger involved."

"But he never did!" Aurelio suddenly broke in.

"How do you know?"

Aurelio was silent. The man went on, "No, he didn't fulfill his intention for the simple reason that a plague broke out among the Indians. They died at a terrible rate. Almost the whole tribe was wiped out. My companion wasn't spared either. I nursed him the best I could for several days. Before he died, he gave me a medallion that he wore. It had belonged to his wife. He was delirious most of the time. But I did understand that he wanted me to find his son and give it to him. I still have the medallion.

"I buried him. Then I left that place before the plague got me too. I'd already survived it once as a child, which was probably why I escaped then. For a while, I tried to find the boy. But my friend had never told me the name of the town.

"One day I learned that the army was after me again. The father had been informed of our desertion, and he was determined to track us down. Not only one daughter had run away from him, but two. The other daughter was presumably caring for the baby.

"I was tired of being constantly hounded from place to place. Eventually, I got down to this part of the world, found it deserted, and decided to stop here. I discovered this island, quite by accident, and it suits me perfectly. Now and again I leave it to buy the few things that I need. I've lost count of the years I've been here. The past all seems like a dream. The present suits me well enough. I have a horse of my own and the stallion for company. He's been coming here, on and off, for a long time too."

He went on to describe to Aurelio how one dark day the stallion had come up from the sea, unbelievably white, unbelievably beautiful. He had hidden in his hut at first, believing him to be a spirit.

"But when he proved himself to be a horse, I stopped hiding and went about my life as usual. It's a small island, but big enough for the pair of us. To-morrow I'll show it to you."

His tale finished, the old gaucho got up and went to tend the fire. He sat staring into the curling smoke and said no more to the boy. Perhaps he was remembering the past again, things he had not spoken out loud. For a while, Aurelio watched him, his heart and mind in turmoil. Then the warmth and comfort overcame him, and he once again lapsed into sleep.

The Indian's Way

The following morning, after a night restless with dreams and emotions, Aurelio told the gray-bearded gaucho his own story. There was a long silence when he had finished. Then the man suddenly pulled a small leather bag from under his belt, and tipped its contents into his hand. There were several coins of copper and silver, and a golden medallion on a fine, crumpled chain. With rough fingers, the gaucho took hold of the delicate object, and handed it over to Aurelio.

"Then this must be yours," he said simply. "I'm glad that I've been able to fulfill my friend's request."

With awe, Aurelio fingered the medallion, which had belonged first to his mother and then to his father. On its face was the figure of the Virgin with a tiny child in her arms. He turned it over and saw written the name *Barbara*, and underneath the date of her birth. At last, he had reached the end of his quest for his father. A strange place it was too—a fogbound island off the Atlantic coast.

The gaucho went outside and left him to ponder over these things. When he returned to the hut, Aurelio was turning the medallion over in his hands, lost in thought. He jumped when the gaucho spoke.

"God has his own ways of leading a man to his goal.

It must be that he meant the stallion to be yours, for it was by following him here that you found what you were seeking. Come outside and see him."

The boy sprang up, but stopped as the gaucho lifted his hand peremptorily.

"Quietly. Slowly. Remember, he's as nervous as the wind."

Aurelio stood silently beside the gaucho in the doorway of the hut. His first sight was of the three horses, his own, the gaucho's, and the stallion, grazing together. All three looked up at him, then after a few seconds returned to their grazing.

Aurelio looked closely at the beautiful stallion. The albino was now in his twelfth year. His body had grown powerfully heavy. Muscles bulged under the thick hair that coated him. His forelock almost hid his eyes, while his tail was so long it almost touched the ground. Aurelio noticed that a twig was caught in it. He had never seen so magnificent an animal. He had to wonder if this were all real, in spite of the wind, in spite of the medallion, warm in his grasp.

The stallion looked up at the boy, his gaze haughty even in its wariness. He tossed his head and whickered and began to move away.

"He knows you don't belong here," said the gaucho.

"If only I could capture him."

The gaucho shook his head. "No one can capture him. You must gain his trust, and hope that he will surrender himself to you. For now, it's best to take no notice of him. I'll show you what there is of the island. Pretend, in the meanwhile, that the stallion doesn't exist."

They mounted their horses and rode from one end of the island to the other, a distance of about a mile. The wind blustered about them, salty and damp. They rode with bowed heads and hunched shoulders. Aurelio's teeth were chattering, and he wondered how his companion could possibly endure such a climate year after year. The mist was thinner that morning. It was possible to see the mainland as a vague shadow beyond the dark, undulating waves. Driftwood and weeds cluttered the island. A flock of gulls hardly disturbed themselves as the horsemen approached.

Aurelio became aware that the white stallion was following them.

"Don't look around," the old gaucho warned him, divining his curiosity. "Let him get to know you in his own way. Remember, this is his island and mine."

It was difficult to resist the temptation, but Aurelio obeyed. They rode slowly around the whole island. The stallion followed, as shy and as curious as a bird. Simmering with excitement, Aurelio forgot the bitterness in the wind.

He wondered at his host's words, doubting their wisdom. How could anyone ever gain the trust of such an animal? How could the horse, of his own accord, surrender himself? The only way to own the stallion was by capturing him and dominating him the way the gauchos had shown him. This old man was a bit queer in the head, which was hardly surprising, considering the life he led. He had come to think of the horse as a person.

Again, the gaucho seemed to guess his thoughts. "You must be patient, very patient. Such an animal as this was never won in a day."

II

Aurelio was patient. He whiled away the hours listening to the old man's stories, asking him questions about his father, and about the horse. While the wind howled and the waves crashed, he learned a good deal about his father, but was left in doubt about the stallion. He knew only one way to break a horse. It was a hard way for him, still not perfectly skilled in equestrian arts. But he felt that sheer pigheadedness would help him to victory in the end, as it had with Bicho.

His host told him that there was another way. When he spoke of gentling the horse instead of breaking him, Aurelio was puzzled and disbelieving. Greater was his disbelief when the gaucho said that it was an art the Indians practiced. The Indians were feared all over the land for their barbarous customs and cruelties. How could they be gentle with a horse?

The gaucho explained how he had seen them still the tossings of the wildest stallion by breathing into its nostrils. It was a common custom for them to "talk" to their horses in this way. They would copy the sounds that the horses made, soft grunts and whickerings that the animals seemed to understand. They would almost immediately lose their fear, and allow a man on their back with hardly a tremble.

"You haven't the strength to beat that stallion into submission," he said to Aurelio. "You must try the Indian's way."

Aurelio tried. Whenever the horse was near, he would talk to it as gently as he could. The stallion would watch him, with pricked ears. After a while the suspicion would fade out of his expression, replaced by curiosity. Never once did Aurelio try to approach the horse. He was as still as a thistle when the wind has dropped. Only his voice went on and on, murmuring soft words and nonsense, until it seemed the stallion was growing to like the sound of it.

He was beginning to think that he was being accepted, and rejoiced with his companion, when the stallion disappeared. For a week he kept away from the island. Aurelio was in despair, first with the horse and then with the weather, which was depressing in the extreme.

"Be patient," the old man continued to counsel him. "The stallion will come back, and he won't have forgotten you." He was used to whiling away his life in this bleak loneliness. It was harder for a lad of seventeen, used to blue skies and sunshine and the wide, green pampa.

The stallion returned. He hung around the hut with the two geldings, watching the boy, listening to him, unable to connect him with the savage, shrieking gauchos that had tormented and terrified him so long ago. There was a rhythm in the soft voice that was pleasant to his ears and no threat in the comparatively small and motionless figure. Aurelio saw that it was as the gaucho had promised him. The stallion lost his caution and had no fear of him.

Following the old man's advice, realizing now that the recluse was not as crazy as he had seemed, Aurelio refrained from touching the horse. He let the stallion see how he fondled his pony and the old gaucho's mount also. The albino saw that neither horse was afraid, and that they even welcomed the boy's attentions. He trembled when the boy mounted his pony and circled him, calmly, silently. His ears were pricked, and it seemed to Aurelio that the animal's brain was digesting the information he was trying to impart.

Though at times he was impatient, wearying of never mounting the beautiful horse, he was glad, too, that the gaucho had shown him this other way of taming a horse. Underneath the callous exterior he had developed during the last two years in self-protection, there was still that sensitive boy who enjoyed the song of a bird and pleasured in the pattern of a rose. To feel that proud animal's body beneath him would be as gratifying as having a skylark perched on his finger. Could such a spirit be subdued? Could so great a confidence grow out of mistrust?

"When can I touch him?" he asked his host. After many times replying, "Not yet, not yet," the old gaucho one day said, "You'll know when the moment is right. Until you know, it will be too soon to touch him."

Aurelio curbed his impatient heart and waited. Spring flowers were pushing themselves up through the few patches of earth on the island. There was even a touch of sunshine, now and again, to break the dark monotony of the days. The stallion came and went. Many times Aurelio would have followed him. Weary of the island, he yearned for the grasslands that seemed but a dream in such a bleak place. He was tired of the stale, roughly cured meat that he lived on, varied occasionally with the tough flesh of a gull. He was tired of the sound of the sea, the sound of the wind, even of the gaucho, who spent long hours in silence and seemed to forget that the boy existed.

After another long absence, Aurelio was determined to make the stallion his. He longed for the albino to return. Eventually, the horse came plunging through the waves, his long mane streaming water. This was the moment.

Aurelio waited just a few yards off, watching while the stallion shook off the water. As he came up the short stretch of beach, Aurelio went forward to meet him, arms outstretched, voice steady and certain.

"Come, beautiful one. You belong to me. You know it. Come. Come."

The stallion came, blowing through his pink nostrils, lowering his head, and touching the boy's hands with his wet muzzle. Aurelio's hand smoothed its way up the sea-soaked head, touching the jaw, the throat, and then his powerful neck. The stallion was still, accepting his touch, blowing through his nostrils, his breath warm on the frozen hand.

For several minutes they stood together thus, the stallion warming the boy with his closeness. Aurelio's sense of triumph was tinged with dread. He had not mounted the horse and was afraid to do so. The moment was too wonderful to lose. If the horse rejected him, he would come no more to the island. Aurelio would never have a second chance to gain his confidence. At the same time, he knew he must go ahead, now, while the horse was consenting. He must be more gentle than the summer wind—but he must be determined.

Summoning all his courage, Aurelio smoothed his way along the stallion's flank. The horse began to jerk his head slightly, as if sensing the boy's inner turmoil. Aurelio was on his back. The stallion jumped, reared slightly, and kicked out his hind legs. But it was a small protest, one that Aurelio could sit out easily, without even clinging. Then the stallion was still. He quivered from withers to rump, as trust in the boy and suddenly-remembered fears conflicted. But there was no pain, no terrifying noise, no force. The trembling died away.

Aurelio forced words from his dry throat, gentle, meaningless words that caused the stallion to prick his ears again and turn them back to catch the sounds. Then he smoothed his hands over the albino's neck. The horse began to move.

He pranced with his high, proud gait; head tossing, nostrils distended, tail lifted. The boy could hardly believe it was a horse he rode. He felt like a god astride a cloud, the rough winds swirling around him. He let the stallion take him where he would, forgetting the existence of everything, even of himself.

He did not see the old gaucho watching him from the doorway of the hut. He was startled back to reality when the stallion danced through the gulls, sending them crying on either side of them. The horse snorted, Aurelio laughed, and the gulls wheeled around them, scolding loudly.

The Return

*When Aurelio and the albino stallion found them-*selves in the land of the ombu tree once again, summer lay heavily over the pampa. The thistles were dry and crackling in the breeze; the ground was hard and taut as a drumhead. Aurelio felt the music in the hoofbeats of his little troop of horses, cantering in solitary state across the deserted plain.. He was riding the albino, the sand stallion. In spite of his stained and dirty clothes and the bare toes that gripped the stirrups, he was king.

Joy overcame pride as his eyes were filled with the sights that had grown so dear to him—the withered grass and bracken, the flocks of birds making dancing, dark patches in the yellow skies, the shining mirage on the horizon of trees and houses. Through his own joy, he recognized a stirring in the stallion, too. The increased effortlessness of his pace, the constantly pricked ears and widened nostrils, surely these were signs of the stallion's gladness to be back in the land that God had given to the gaucho and his ponies.

Aurelio and the stallion had come to know each other well in the few weeks that they had traveled together. From their long association on the island, Aurelio's heart had expanded into love for this wild creature that had come to put his trust in him.

When they halted for the night, the horses grazed together not far from Aurelio's resting place, hobbled, except for the stallion. There were times when he believed that he would wake up to find the albino gone. He disdained haltering the legs of this wild one, for he felt he had no right to call the stallion his. If one day, he chose to desert him, called again to the liberty he had forsaken, Aurelio knew that greater than regret and sorrow would be the privilege of having once ridden him and exercised a calming influence over him.

Sometimes, he almost wanted him to go, feeling that he was not entitled to cling to him as a piece of personal property. When the stallion stayed, in spite of the winds and the smells and the sounds that teased him, Aurelio's love for him grew greater.

He did not know why the stallion stayed. One night, when the moon was so bright that he could not sleep, he watched the albino, whiter than ever in the silver-lit darkness. His head and shoulders comfortably resting against the saddle, his fingers absently twisting the gold medallion around his neck, he saw how the stallion sought out the different scents, body alternately taut or quivering. Never had he realized until that moment how wild he really was, forgetful now of the boy who held sway over his instincts. Why did he not go? Why did he stay when every breath of wind tormented him?

He wanted him to go, to be free, galloping tracelessly over the land that belonged to him. The boy's conscience was heavy. With Indian wile, he had made this essentially free creature his slave.

It was in one of these pensive moments that Aurelio

remembered the vow he had made in the shepherd's hut, to return to the pampa only when he could bring back the sand stallion as a gift for the majordomo. He had no right to give this horse to another person, any more than he had the right to take it for himself. But a vow was a vow, he could not escape it.

In spite of this, he smiled when he remembered Serafin, who had always been around to give advice when it was needed and to mock him when he grew presumptuous. Surely there was no better person to whom he could give the stallion. He was understanding, for all that he was rough, and cared well for his favorite mounts.

Remembering, Aurelio knew that he still wanted to give the stallion to him. But he ached to think of parting with the horse. How else could he show the majordomo that he was grateful for all that he had done for him? He knew that the gaucho wanted no thanks for having saved his life. He knew, too, that only by sacrificing something dear of his own could he ever repay him.

In the days that were left to them, Aurelio greatly cherished the white stallion. He continued to fill the sharply pricked ears with the sound of his voice; he even learned—shyly at first—to breathe into the stallion's big nostrils, wondering if the animal way of communicating would bring them closer.

The stallion was still his powerful, haughty self, but the boy, with gentleness, had reached the docility that was also within him. Essentially a gregarious animal, the undemanding friendship the boy offered him after his long isolation was all he needed to subdue his mistrust of mankind and sublimate his instinctive fear. He did not even quiver when the boy sat astride him, knowing that no harm would come from him. He had no sense of being captive, for he had come of his own accord. Though the winds spoke of space and liberty, the stallion lacked neither. He rejoiced in the early summer smells, and he rejoiced in his companion.

Aurelio felt the joy that was in the stallion. But his heart was sometimes heavy. Was he not betraying the stallion, taking him to Santa Clara?

II

The young son of one of the gauchos who worked at Santa Clara was whiling away the afternoon, standing on his pony's back and watching the horizon. Both boy and pony had been as still as a reed on a windless day for a long time. The pony was asleep, but its ears automatically twitched as the sound of hurrying hooves reached them. The boy saw the slight movement and continued his watch with more emotion. Something, or someone, was coming, though not yet in sight. He waited until a few specks appeared on the yellow horizon. Then he thumped into the saddle by opening his legs, waking the pony with a start. He dashed back to the ranch house, calling to its owner.

"Someone's coming, Don Jacinto. Someone's coming. A man with four horses, Don Jacinto."

Several dogs began to bark. A couple of tethered horses moved restlessly. But Don Jacinto was asleep, and so profoundly that even the three flies crawling on his face did not disturb him.

Action was the only antidote to the tedious afternoon. The boy raced off to where the gauchos were
herding, followed by a crowd of dogs. The boy's father
told the majordomo. Serafin left someone else in
charge, took a fresh horse, and returned to the estancia
to await the traveler. It was probably a gaucho looking
for work, and Don Jacinto would be annoyed if waked
for such a detail.

Thus it was that when Aurelio arrived there was
none but the majordomo to greet him. The boy halted
the stallion a hundred yards from the gateposts—the
only sign that suggested that here the pampa stopped
for a while and civilization began—too embarrassed
now to approach the man he had longed to see. He was
sure that the gaucho would ridicule him for his pre-
sumption in taking up his last-flung challenge, and,
worse still, succeeding.

The majordomo's face was impassive. But it was he
who urged his own splendid horse forward and rode to
greet the returning boy.

He halted a length's distance away, and sat back in
the saddle to admire the stallion. The albino grew
nervous at the man's proximity. He pawed the ground
and tossed his head, his anxious hooves beginning to
dance. Aurelio uttered a few soft words and stilled
him.

"Well, you've come back," said the majordomo at
last. "I thought you'd forgotten us." Both his tone and
glance were laconic, crushing the enthusiasm Aurelio
felt at the longed-for sight of him. "I see you've come
back with a new horse."

"It's the sand stallion. You told me to look for him.
That's why I've been so long." There was a mixture of

anger and righteous pride in the boy's voice.

"So you return more gaucho than all of us. Congratulations!"

"It's for you. For the one that died. I only found him for you."

Unexpectedly, he recognized a glint in the gaucho's black eyes, and realized that Serafin was teasing him all along. Overwhelmed with relief, a childish grin spread over his more manly features.

"Get down from there," shouted the majordomo, "so I can see if you've grown or not. It's probably only the horse that makes you look like a man."

They dismounted simultaneously. Aurelio was surprised to find himself being tightly hugged.

"I haven't slept a peaceful night since I left you with the shepherd," confessed Serafin gruffly as he released Aurelio. "I knew what you'd be up to, arrogant pup that you are."

With these words, Aurelio understood that everything was all right again between them. Had he not been so depressed by his own defeat last autumn, he would have realized then that Serafin's friendship was not so easily won . . . or lost.

It was another lesson in humility, but one that he could take without smarting. At last, he realized how presumptuous and young he had been. All the time at Santa Clara, and later in his pursuit of the stallion, he had wanted to be a gaucho. He never realized until now that it was more important to prove himself a man first. He could not be a gaucho without being a man. This was what Serafin had been trying to teach him all along.

Serafin studied the stallion. He watched the albino's

eyes, how they rested on the youth. Something in the look was familiar to him. There was no wildness, no mistrust. It was questioning, eager, expectant—the look he had often found in the eyes of his own favorite horse.

He could not help wondering how a mere youth could dominate this powerful savage, so strong in his years and much larger than the average pony. He concluded that it was not physical force that had wrought the wildness from the stallion.

"Is that horse really broken? Can anyone ride him, or is it just your magic touch that controls him?"

The old irony was in his words, but Aurelio was no longer sensitive to it. Now he accepted it for what it was worth, a challenge.

"I don't know. He answers well enough to heel and rein. I don't know how he'll behave with another person."

"Can I try him?"

"He's yours!"

Serafin stared shrewdly at him. This time Aurelio was able to meet his look with new understanding.

For days, he had been trying to think of a way of telling the gaucho to be gentle with the horse. Without offending him, he wanted to tell him to use no whip or spurs. There was no need to speak at all.

Aurelio stood in front of the stallion, holding the bridle. The gaucho approached and smoothed his hand along the restless neck, speaking softly to the horse all the while. Gathering up the reins in a nonchalant manner, he was instantly in the saddle, relaxed but vigilant. The albino tossed his head and flattened his ears. Aurelio let go of the bridle.

"Let's see how he runs," said the gaucho.

He touched the stallion's flanks lightly with his spurs. The horse reared, then sprang into a gallop. He ran fearlessly and with a grace that was beautiful to behold. The gaucho gave him his head.

Aurelio was left at the gateposts with the major-domo's horse. It was a strange sensation for him to watch the stallion and the gaucho. The albino cantered, his head high, his tail a banner in the breeze. Serafin seemed a part of the stallion, his body moving in exact rhythm with that of his steed. They belonged together.

Serafin sprang from the saddle before the stallion had drawn to a halt. He dropped the reins into Aurelio's hands and grinned at him.

"What a ride! Tame as a lamb! I thought you said this was the sand stallion. Here, take him. You'd better collect your other horses too. There's some herding to be done. I've wasted enough of the afternoon already."

The stallion stood a while, blowing and shaking his head, his eager hooves still printing the grass. Aurelio mounted him and rode back for Lucero and the two geldings. He did not know what to make of the gaucho's words, unable to believe he was actually refusing the gift.

As he returned to the rancho, he recognized one of the horses half-dozing in the nearby corral. Surely that mealy-colored creature with the swollen joints and the rheumy eyes was his old Mouse! His heart flooded with affection at the sight of him. Suddenly, he remembered how he had first ridden up to Santa Clara on the feeble animal. He had learned a lot since that long-ago day. Now he rode a full-blooded stallion that many a man had wanted to possess.

He would have gone up to the horse and called to him, but Serafin was growing impatient. He had no time for such an overflow of sentiment.

"Come on! Shake up that bag of bones you're riding."

"But don't you want him?" Aurelio asked incredulously. "I brought him for you."

He said it with true humility this time. He had learned there was no pride between friends.

"We both lost a horse that day," Serafin reminded him. "Don't be so anxious to give him away. Besides, I've had my share of beautiful horses."

He spurred his mount and galloped off in the direction of the herders, looking back at Aurelio and waving him to follow.

He shouted, "Let him teach you how to ride, boy. He'll make a gaucho of you yet."

The stallion was only waiting for Aurelio to give him his head. He flung himself after the advancing figures, and Aurelio and the gaucho were soon abreast. The gaucho shouted and spurred his horse on. Aurelio was taunted by his teasing and did the same. At once both horses were stretched out in headlong gallop, their riders encouraging them with yells of delight.

Old Mouse in the corral pricked his ears, disturbed by the tempo of their hooves. Then he returned to dozing in the sunshine, which was all that he was good for now.